"Damn Red Rose," Parker whispered.

He stared down at Ellie and saw that her eyes were wide and worried, her lips parted slightly.

"You should be married," he said. "You should have babies. If I help you, that'll happen. Getting husbands and babies for all of you.... That's what this is all about, anyway, isn't it?"

She shook her head vehemently. "Not for me. I don't want a husband."

"So, this isn't about husbands?"

"It is. Just not about mine. I'd like to see my friends and maybe even some of my sisters happily married. Do you think there is such a thing as a happy marriage?"

"For some. Not for me. I love women, but for me there's only friendship, there's only..."

"Sex?" she asked, wide-eyed.

"Well, not always sex," Parker whispered, leaning close. "Sometimes there's just friendship, or kissing, or sometimes friendship *and* kissing."

And if she hadn't been Ellie, if he hadn't promised himself years ago never to go near her, he might have demonstrated.

Dear Reader,

April showers are bringing flowers—and a soul-stirring bouquet of dream-come-true stories from Silhouette Romance!

Red Rose needs men! And it's up to Ellie Donahue to put the town-ladies' plans into action—even if it means enticing her secret love to return to his former home. Inspired by classic legends, Myrna Mackenzie's new miniseries, THE BRIDES OF RED ROSE, begins with Ellie's tale, in *The Pied Piper's Bride* (SR #1714).

Bestselling author Judy Christenberry brings you another Wild West story in her FROM THE CIRCLE K miniseries. In *The Last Crawford Bachelor* (SR #1715), lawyer Michael Crawford—the family's last single son—meets his match…and is then forced to live with her on the Circle K!

And this lively bunch of spring stories wouldn't be complete without Teresa Carpenter's *Daddy's Little Memento* (SR #1716). School nurse Samantha Dell reunites her infant nephew with his handsome father, only to learn that if she wants to retain custody then she's got to say, "I do"! And then there's Colleen Faulkner's *Barefoot and Pregnant?* (SR #1717), in which career-woman Elise Montgomery has everything a girl could want—except the man of her dreams. Will she find a husband where she least expects him?

All the best,

Mavis C. Allen
Associate Senior Editor

Please address questions and book requests to:
Silhouette Reader Service
U.S.: 3010 Walden Ave., P.O. Box 1325, Buffalo, NY 14269
Canadian: P.O. Box 609, Fort Erie, Ont. L2A 5X3

The Pied Piper's Bride

MYRNA MACKENZIE

Published by Silhouette Books
America's Publisher of Contemporary Romance

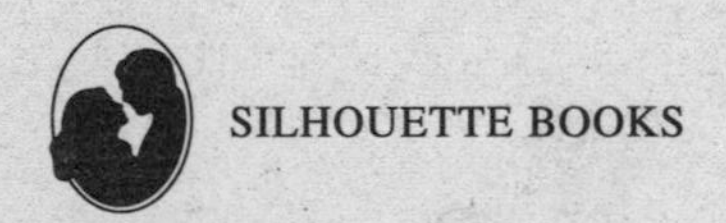

ISBN 0-373-19714-4

THE PIED PIPER'S BRIDE

This edition published by arrangement with Harlequin Books S.A.

Visit Silhouette at www.eHarlequin.com

Printed in U.S.A.

Books by Myrna Mackenzie

Silhouette Romance

The Baby Wish #1046
The Daddy List #1090
Babies and a Blue-Eyed Man #1182
The Secret Groom #1225
The Scandalous Return of Jake Walker #1256
Prince Charming's Return #1361
**Simon Says... Marry Me!* #1429
**At the Billionaire's Bidding* #1442
**Contractually His* #1454
The Billionaire Is Back #1520
Blind-Date Bride #1526
A Very Special Delivery #1540
**Bought by the Billionaire* #1610
**The Billionaire's Bargain* #1622
**The Billionaire Borrows a Bride* #1634
†*The Pied Piper's Bride* #1714

*The Wedding Auction
†The Brides of Red Rose

Silhouette Books

Montana Mavericks
Just Pretending

Lone Star Country Club
Her Sweet Talkin' Man

Baby and All
Lights, Camera... Baby!

MYRNA MACKENZIE,

winner of the Holt Medallion honoring outstanding literary talent, believes that there are many unsung heroes and heroines living among us, and she loves to write about such people. She tries to inject her characters with humor, loyalty and honor, and after many years of writing she is still thrilled to be able to say that she makes her living by daydreaming. Myrna lives with her husband and two sons in the suburbs of Chicago. During the summer she likes to take long walks, and during cold Chicago winters, she likes to *think* about taking long walks (or dream of summers in Maine). Readers may write to Myrna at P.O. Box 225, LaGrange, IL 60525, or they may visit her online at www.myrnamackenzie.com.

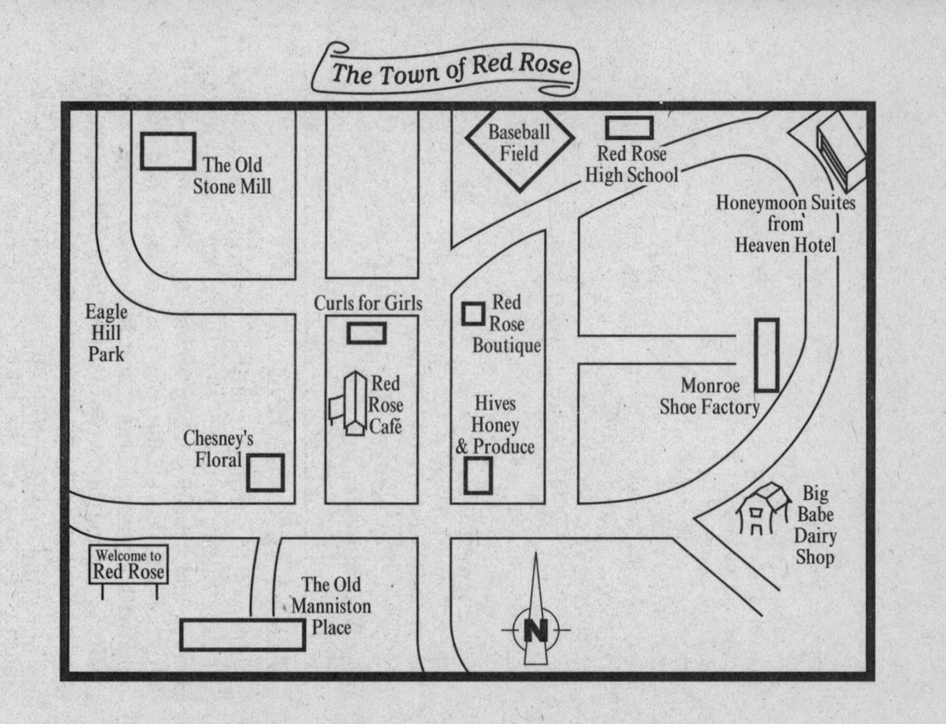
The Town of Red Rose
The Old Stone Mill
Baseball Field
Red Rose High School
Honeymoon Suites from Heaven Hotel
Eagle Hill Park
Curls for Girls
Red Rose Boutique
Red Rose Café
Hives Honey & Produce
Monroe Shoe Factory
Chesney's Floral
Big Babe Dairy Shop
Welcome to Red Rose
The Old Manniston Place
N

Chapter One

"I'm so frustrated that if a man doesn't wander into town soon, I'm going out to the highway, lasso one and throw him over my shoulder."

Ellie Donahue grinned at the comment her robust friend, Sunny, had thrown out. "Let's not get crazy, Sunny. Besides, who really needs a man? This early in the morning you just need another cup of coffee." She poured her friend another cup. "This one's on me."

Her last comment was directed to both Sunny and Lydia. Lydia was a sixtyish silver-haired woman and the owner of the Red Rose Café where Ellie was filling in, waiting tables during the breakfast rush.

Lydia chortled. "No, it's on me. And Ellie, honey, she's right. We *all* need a man. This town could use a whole lot of men, seeing as how we pretty much don't have any."

Ellie opened her mouth, and Rosellen January, who ran the drug store and was close to six feet tall, held up her hand. "Don't even mention Brady or Caleb or Mister Fipps, Ellie. You know what Lydia means. I want a man who's willing to talk to me, who'll still be in my bed when the morning comes and who's under ninety-five years of age. Red Rose doesn't have anyone like that anymore. The young men leave as soon as they can get out and support themselves, and the few that stay are too unmotivated and lazy to do anything, much less be good providers and husbands."

Ellie shrugged and sat down at the table next to her friends. "Red Rose is still home."

"Yes, but our home is dying," Joyce Hives said softly, playing with the tail of her light brown braid. "Rural small-town Illinois has its charms, but in this case, we're getting so small that soon there won't be anything left of us. We've dropped to less than three thousand people and falling. The population marker at the edge of town could be changed every six months and it still wouldn't be right."

"That's right. If I don't get some business over at the dairy shop soon, my profits are going to dry up completely and I'm going to have to close the doors. And if I don't get a man in my bed, *I'm* going to dry up and disappear. Don't you ever feel that way, Ellie?" Sunny frowned at her coffee cup.

Ellie was glad that she'd never had the tendency to blush. She knew what Sunny was talking about. At twenty-nine, she'd heard plenty about the kind of heat that was supposed to be generated between a man and a woman, but her early experiences in life must have put her on the wrong track. Her mother had given birth to seven babies within ten years, all before her twenty-ninth birthday and all difficult pregnancies and births. A frail and nervous woman, Luann Donahue's childbirth and mothering experiences had left her worn out before she'd even lived, and Ellie's own experiences with men, few as they were, had been awful. There had been her father, who had never taken any interest in his children. He had been positively cruel to his wife until the day he died when Ellie was nine. There had also been Gunther Thurlo, who had purported to be Ellie's friend when she was nineteen, but who had tried to rip her dress and had called her names when she wouldn't sleep with him. And three years later, there had been Avery Johns, who had wanted her only to take care of his four motherless children, to give him even more children, and who had run out and proposed to another woman the day after Ellie had told him no. In her world, relationships with men always turned out wrong, no matter how promising they looked at first glance.

Two of her sisters, Lana and Ronnie, had stayed in Red Rose, married young and were already divorced, while their husbands moved on. Her other four sisters, Allie, the twins Becca and Judy, and Suze had gone away to college and never returned. None of them seemed to have much interest in marriage. So Ellie was positive the kind of stuff Sunny was referring to was only appealing on the big screen. Men and marriage didn't offer anything she wanted badly enough to go through the hell she'd seen her mother and sisters go through, and she was just glad that she could support herself.

"But I do want Red Rose to survive," she said gently, ignoring Sunny's question.

"Well, it won't if we can't bring in new blood,"

Lydia warned. "We're all hurting, every business in town. Like it or not, Ellie, Red Rose needs men. The kind of men that can rejuvenate and repopulate our town."

"So what do we do?" Ellie heard herself ask the question with a definite sense of déjà vu. This conversation had been repeated before, but before things had not been this serious. She knew Sunny and Lydia were right. The economy of Red Rose had taken a hit in the past couple of years. The town wasn't just suffering from a shortage of men. Half the small group of kids who had graduated from Red Rose High just a month ago had already wandered north to Chicago looking for the things that Red Rose could no longer provide. In a town of less than three thousand, with no industry, there just wasn't anything to keep an ambitious young man here. For every four women there was only one man, and a significant number of the men were either very old or too young to leave.

"We could have a big party and hope that some of the guys from neighboring towns show up and stay," Delia Sable, a young and pretty blue-eyed blonde who worked at Chesney's Floral volunteered.

"Did that," Lydia answered. "They ate our food and drank a lot of beer, but in the end they went home."

"We could build something that would attract attention to Red Rose and bring in tourists," Joyce Hives said.

Ellie smiled sadly. "We did that, too, remember?" She almost shuddered to think of the hideous statue sitting at the edge of the highway on the far side of town.

"We need something more solid," Sunny declared.

"We need someone who knows what men want and who has the money and the clout to bring them here," Lydia agreed. "What we need is a business consultant."

"Well, yes, that does make sense, I suppose," Ellie said.

"You know, Parker Monroe is a consultant. Helps businesses match up with new markets," Sunny said slowly, staring pointedly at Ellie. "I read that in a special 'People Who Make the City Work' section of the *Chicago Tribune.*"

Ellie suddenly felt her breath sticking in her throat. She had a very bad feeling about where this conversation was headed. "I hardly think Parker is going to come back to Red Rose," she said. "It's been eleven years since he left town, and he didn't leave smiling."

"He might come back for a visit if it was put to him in the right way," Lydia mused. "You knew him pretty well once, didn't you?"

The lump in Ellie's throat grew larger. "I was eighteen when he left." And she had hidden that day, unwilling and unable to say goodbye to a man who had barely even known she was alive.

"But you were friends."

"Only as youngsters. When we started growing up and leaving childhood behind, we were more like acquaintances." Only in her girlish dreams had they been more. And that had been before she'd made up her mind about men. She was older and more knowledgeable these days. She wouldn't be susceptible to Parker's charms now. Still…

"You lived next door to the Monroes. Your mother was their cook."

Ellie nodded. Her home, had, in fact, once been the

servants' quarters for the Monroe estate before Parker's grandfather had willed it to Ellie's grandmother, who had been the Monroe's cook before Ellie's mother had taken over.

"And you're so good at getting things done, Ellie. Look at the way you always step in here to help out when I need an extra hand during breakfast." Lydia knew just how to make a point.

"And you fixed my plumbing last week for thirty dollars when that guy over in Lenoxton was going to charge me seventy-five." Joyce smiled sweetly.

"Yes, you do it all, Ellie. You know how to hang wallpaper and paint and fix electrical messes. You're the ticket agent for the bus line, you baby-sit when someone needs you to, and most of all, you don't take nonsense. From anyone. You're strong and persistent, you take care of us, you're...convincing."

Delia finished up and all eyes turned Ellie's way.

"She's right. Parker might help us if you talked to him, Ellie," Sunny said keeping her huge blue eyes on Ellie.

Ellie shook her head and held out her hands. "Why would he come? And what would he do here? How could even the best consultant attract business to a dying town?"

"Even if you could only get him to come here for a few weeks or days, he's rich and famous. He was the first influential man to leave Red Rose. If he came back, maybe people would notice us and they'd follow him in here just the way they followed him out." Sunny pressed on.

"They didn't follow him out."

"Well, they left after his daddy closed down the shoe factory—it was the only one in the country Mick

Monroe closed—and that was right before he died and right after Parker left.''

''The plant was losing money like crazy. The Monroes made their money buying small firms, hiring people to make them into big ones and then selling high, but if something went wrong, they got out,'' Ellie pointed out. The shoe factory had been one of Mick Monroe's few ''from scratch'' projects.

''If Parker had come back, his daddy might have asked him to run the factory. Then Mick might not have closed it, and he might have made it pay. And anyway, even if Mick had gone ahead and shut it down, Parker could have come back and reopened the plant after his daddy died.''

''He's a man, not a magician, Joyce, and no one, Parker included, could have saved the shoe factory. Besides, he was only twenty-one when he left here, barely twenty-two when Mick died.''

''He was a Monroe.''

Which appeared to say it all for everyone. The Monroes had been the only millionaires ever to live in Red Rose. Ergo, they must know secrets that the rest of the world didn't.

Ellie frowned. ''You can't seriously think Parker was the reason the town began to lose its male population. Surely we're not that superstitious.''

No one answered. Whether they thought Parker had wronged them by not reopening the factory or whether they simply thought of him as a symbol for the exodus of men in the ensuing years, it was clear that everyone considered Parker to be intimately tied to their problems, both as villain and savior. Ellie sighed. ''How do you expect me to get him here?''

''Bait,'' Lydia said.

Panic blossomed in Ellie's chest. ''Bait?''

Sunny nodded.

''What would I use for bait?''

''He likes beautiful women,'' Sunny said. ''I get both the Chicago papers, and his picture's always in the society pages with a different woman. Just…fix yourself up. Wear more makeup. Wear fewer clothes. Get Annie over at Curls for Girls to fix your hair in the latest style.''

''Absolutely not.''

''Please, Ellie. We need you. You've always helped us before. I've…I've only ever even been kissed once in my life.'' Delia's voice wobbled. Big tears formed on her lashes.

Ellie tried not to let her own distress show. She had once had a tremendous crush on Parker. True, she'd barely turned eighteen when he left while he was well into his twenty-first year, but she'd had feelings for him for years and he'd never even looked at her as if she were female. She had felt helpless, hopeless, and she didn't want those old feelings to resurface. She'd always worried that he might discover her secret….

''I'm sorry, but I just can't play go-between with Parker for you,'' she told her friends. ''It's out of the question. Completely impossible. Can't be done. Ever.''

Parker Monroe put his feet up on his desk and leaned back in his chair, contemplating his upcoming business trip to Europe. It was going to be good to fade into the anonymity of a foreign country, a place where no one knew his face or his reputation.

These past weeks had been difficult. He'd been so

focused on his work that he hadn't realized that Lynette was starting to hear wedding bells. And then he *had* realized, and everything had gone to pieces. She'd told him that she knew better than to hope, but she'd lost her focus, too. He'd hurt her, unwittingly but irrevocably, and then she'd stormed out. The break had been very public. The newspapers hadn't left him alone for days. His conscience had hounded him much longer.

He'd known all his adult life that he would never marry. The Monroe men didn't have a faithful bone in their collective bodies, and he had no interest in following in his father's, or his uncle's, or his grandfather's footsteps; marrying women and then ruining their lives. When he'd been young, he thought he might be different. That he might fall in love for real, but he'd only ended up trying and failing and hurting women over and over. Now he'd gotten set in his ways. He liked the single life and didn't want to change. He'd thought he'd made it clear to Lynette that marriage wasn't an option, but apparently he hadn't been clear enough. He'd gotten careless, and careless wasn't allowed for a man like him.

So yes, he was going to love getting out of town, even if it was only for business. He needed a place where he could gain perspective, and he couldn't do that in the States where his name was so well known. *Especially* not here, the scene of his crime. It occurred to him that he was beginning to have too many "crime scenes" in his life. First Red Rose, now Chicago. He definitely needed to get away for a while.

A buzzer broke into his thoughts, and Parker jabbed at the button on the arm of his chair. "Yes?"

"Someone to see you, Parker. A Ms. Donahue. She

says it's about a rather tricky consulting job. She's not sure you can handle it. Should I send her away?''

Parker grinned. The woman's technique was clearly a ploy. He didn't take walk-in jobs anymore, and everyone knew that. But in his present disgruntled state, he was in the mood for a tussle, and he admired someone who would buck the odds and attempt to outmaneuver him. Even though he didn't anticipate taking the job this Ms. Donahue was here about, he had to admire someone with the guts to come in person and try to hoodwink him. A little mental sparring might be fun.

''Send her in, Jeb.''

''Excuse me?''

''Open the door, man. I'm available. For the next five minutes, anyway.''

''If you say so, Parker.''

Jeb's voice had barely died away and Parker had just had the chance to stand, his palms resting on his desk, when the door slipped open a crack and a slender woman squeezed through. She appeared to stop and take a deep breath for a second. But that must have been his imagination, because in the next second she was charging forward, her hand outstretched, a look of stalwart determination in her solemn, gray eyes.

''Good afternoon, Parker. I'll try not to take up too much of your time. As I mentioned to your…'' She glanced over her shoulder to the room where Jeb had been.

Parker grinned. ''My receptionist. Jeb is my receptionist.'' But he could understand her consternation. Everyone reacted that way to Jeb. The man had played college football, and his body had the dimensions of a small tank. He looked like a bouncer—and sometimes he was.

"Yes, as I mentioned to your receptionist," she repeated, more calmly, "I doubt you'll be able to help me."

This was getting interesting right away, in more ways than one if his eyes and his memory weren't deceiving him. "Then why are you here?"

The woman raised her head slightly, as if forcing herself to be brave. This time she definitely took a deep breath, no question. Like a dignified little gray mouse, she pulled back those slender shoulders in that mannish and out-of-style charcoal suit she wore, she lifted her chin even higher and directed her cool gaze at him.

There was something about those eyes, something much older than her years suggested. Something all too familiar and distressing.

"I promised Red Rose I'd come, Parker, so here I am. I'm hoping you can help us. I really am, or I would never be here at all."

Ah, so he had been right about the memories. She was from Red Rose. But then, he'd known that, hadn't he? Ellie wasn't the kind of person you forgot.

Parker closed his eyes, and there she was in his mind, still gazing at him with those clear gray eyes. A much younger version of the woman standing here in his office today. A girl he hadn't wanted to remember. Because he was sure he'd hurt her, the way the men in his family always hurt women, unintentionally or otherwise. Like it or not, the Monroe men were shallow, incapable of much beyond making money, and that wasn't what any woman wanted to hear. He'd earned his guilty conscience, he'd hidden from it, but here it was, standing before him. His past had reached forward and caught him today, it seemed.

Shaking his head, Parker pushed away the image and really looked at the woman. Hard this time. He came out from behind his desk and walked around her, circled her. She wasn't much bigger than she had been the last time he'd seen her, but there was something very different. A veneer, a wariness, maybc even a hint of an edge. She was still tiny, her eyes still too big for her face, her demeanor still as solemn, but now there was a dignity that had been missing last time, a wall. There was something about the way she held her body rigid and tight that said, ''Don't even try to snow me, buddy. I know you.'' And she did. A bit.

''Ellie?'' he asked incredulously. ''Is it really Ellie Donahue?''

''You didn't know.'' The veneer shattered just a bit. ''Your receptionist...I told him. I said...'' She thought back and then she grimaced. ''Well, I suppose Donahue is a rather common name, at least in Chicago.''

''Just in Chicago?''

Finally, he surprised a slight smile. ''All right, there used to be a lot of us in Red Rose, too, before some of my sisters moved away. My father saw to that.''

''I'm just...perplexed. You came all the way from Red Rose to see me?''

She frowned. ''It's only a few hours' drive.''

But one which no one from his hometown had ever made before. At least not to see him. He raised a brow, questioning.

She folded her hands primly in front of her, right

beneath her breasts. In spite of the awful suit, it was clear that Ellie Donahue had grown up in several ways during the past eleven years. She'd apparently been a late bloomer, still coltish and angular when he'd gone. Now there were definite well-defined curves beneath the bulky material. Softly rounded breasts which refused to be hidden, and shapely legs beneath the hem of her skirt. Yes, Ellie had blossomed into a woman with some attractive features, all right, which was really just none of his damn business.

He cleared his throat and refused to let his eyes wander any farther.

Ellie looked directly up at him, her jaw taut, her fingers laced tightly together. "I know it's presumptuous of me to ask, but Red Rose needs your help."

"My help?"

She stood a little straighter, a little taller. "Yes."

"Ellie, you're joking. Why are you really here?"

She widened her eyes. "Joking?"

Right. She never joked. At least she hadn't when she'd been a girl. She'd been far too serious, he'd always thought. Life was just bound to hurt someone that intense.

"Um...Ellic? Did you really say that Red Rose needs my help? Maybe you've forgotten what was going on just before I left Red Rose."

She shook her head slowly, sucking in her bottom lip. The gesture was completely innocent, which was no doubt why it socked him in the gut so hard when he felt a flicker of desire slip in where it had no business going.

"I remember," she said. "My cousin Mitzi accused you of being the father of her child. My Uncle Cliff believed her, and he wanted you to marry her.''

For a moment he was back in Red Rose. He was twenty-one and standing in a room filled with men and women glaring at him. Anger filled his heart, but there was also a sense that maybe he deserved that animosity. He hadn't impregnated Mitzi, who was a regular visitor at the Donahue's house, but he had done other things and would do more if he stayed.

''You agreed to marry her, even though the baby wasn't yours,'' she said, her eyes wide.

Parker shrugged. ''Don't make me out to be more than I am. I agreed to marry Mitzi in a moment of cowardice.''

Ellie raised one delicate shoulder and cocked her head. ''Really? You're a full head taller than my Uncle Cliff and in a lot better shape, even when he's sober, which is rare. I think you just felt sorry for her.''

She was wrong. He *had* felt sorry for Mitzi, who had clearly been scared out of her wits. But the reason he had agreed to the marriage had been simply a matter of anger and defiance. Not at her uncle, but at himself. His father had forged a reputation as a wealthy ne'er do well who cared nothing for anyone but his own comforts, and he, the Monroe heir, had carried on the family ways, moving from one girl to the next, uninvolved beyond a surface level. Parker had known he was leaving a trail of hurt feelings behind him. He'd regretted it, tried to prevent it with youthful honesty, which never seemed to work. His inability to offer meaningful promises or love to a woman had never been a matter of pride, but a weakness he recognized, one he detested, especially whenever he looked at his mother and saw how her life had been ruined by the same sort of selfish man.

She'd always warned Parker that some day a man would have to pay for his sins, so when Mitzi had accused him of impregnating her, he had considered her lie to be simply his due, almost a relief. "Well," he said, his voice devoid of all expression, "my actions were moot once Mitzi's boyfriend stepped forward, indignant that some other man would be stealing his bride and baby."

"And then you left town."

He shrugged. "It was past time, anyway. You understand, Ellie, that I left town for good?"

She seemed to study him for a second. Then she firmed her mouth and gave a curt nod as if coming to a decision. She stepped forward. "I know that you never intended to return, but maybe you didn't know, maybe you still don't know what your leaving did to Red Rose."

Parker raised an inquiring brow. "I'm guessing you're going to inform me?" He managed to smile, though he was wildly curious to see what Ellie was going to come up with. He'd been right before. This was going to be interesting.

She lifted her chin. "After you left town, all the other men started trickling out."

"Really? You think they followed me?"

Her lids fluttered. "Not exactly, but after you left, your father closed the factory. The men began leaving for the city. You started something that hasn't stopped."

Parker leaned back against his desk and stared down at Ellie, less than a foot away from her now. The scent of wild roses drifted to him. He pretended he didn't notice. "Ellie, I couldn't have stopped the closing of the plant if I'd tried, and I haven't been secretly luring the men of Red Rose to Chicago. They're not all staying at my house," he teased.

She raised her head suddenly, her jaw tense, her eyes angry. "I know that. I'm not a little girl anymore, Parker. The point is that Red Rose is losing people, mostly men. The town is dying."

"And I started the exodus."

She glanced down, breaking contact with him for the first time. "In a way, maybe just in a symbolic sort of way. It doesn't really matter whether you started something or whether the women of Red Rose simply think you did. The town is falling apart, and we need your help to stop it."

"Ellie, you can't believe that that's possible. This isn't like when we were kids and you asked me to round up the bad guys and tie them to the oak tree."

"I don't want you to round up the bad guys and I don't want you to play. I want you to come back to Red Rose and see what can be done to save the town."

"I'm a businessman, Ellie, not a miracle worker."

"You're a very successful businessman in a field that could benefit us. You could try."

"I'm a successful businessman because I don't take on doomed projects. This one wouldn't work, and I don't think I want to go back and make a fruitless attempt at saving the town I left. Red Rose is behind me."

"You don't believe anyone still thinks you're the father of Mitzi's son?"

Parker chuckled. "Not at all. I saw a picture once.

The boy doesn't look like me at all. Monroes have very aristocratic noses, you know,'' he teased.

She smiled then, fully for the first time, her face brightening up his office. It was an old joke. He'd broken his nose once, falling from that same oak tree, and his mother had fretted for days about the possibility that he had ruined the Monroe claim to fame.

''You could make an exception, make an attempt,'' she said softly.

''No, Red Rose was dying long before I left, Ellie.''

''I know.''

It was his turn to blink. ''You know there's not much hope, but—''

She shrugged, silencing him. ''The women of Red Rose think you can help. Sometimes that's all it takes to effect change. A little hope, a little confidence.''

''It would take a miracle to save Red Rose. You don't still believe in miracles, do you, Ellie?''

She shook her head. ''No, I don't. But I can't give up on Red Rose. I have to try. I hoped you'd try, too.''

''I'm sorry, Ellie. Red Rose is far in my past. I left it behind long ago, and I rather like it that way.''

She blew out a breath that lifted her bangs from her forehead. ''I knew you were going to be stubborn. You always were, you know?''

He grinned. ''I know.'' She'd told him that before when she'd been eleven and he fourteen and she had come up with some dreamer of a scheme to change the world and he'd shot holes through it in his cocky fourteen-year-old male way.

''I refuse to give up on Red Rose.''

''Don't give up on Red Rose, Ellie. It's your home. It's just not mine.''

She put her hands on her hips, a move she'd used even as a child. It had been cute back then. Now, the way it emphasized her hips and the thrust of her breasts, it was delicious. She probably didn't know that.

''Sunny Delavan told me the way to convince you was to appeal to your basic senses,'' Ellie said, shaking her head. ''She suggested I come in here wearing a lacy bikini with a push-up bra. Would that have helped?''

For a moment Parker felt as if his brain had received an electric shock that rendered all rational thought impossible. The thought of sweet little serious Ellie coming in here dressed in a barely there outfit that would expose the full length of those silky legs and emphasize those rounded curves that were hidden beneath layers of cloth right now was ludicrous...and exciting as hell.

''Don't come back, Ellie,'' he said suddenly, his voice rasping slightly. ''Especially don't come back dressed to kill. You remember my father?''

She took a deep breath and nodded. ''Of course.''

''I'm just like him, Ellie. I'm worse than him, worse even than my Uncle Fitz who was married eight times, and I'm not to be trusted with a woman's body. Remember that.''

For a moment he thought he saw her shiver and take a step back. Good. He had scared her just enough to protect her.

But as she turned to go out the door, she looked back over her shoulder. ''I'm sorry, I can't give up, Parker. Red Rose is my home and I have to fight for it and for the people I love. I don't want to be a pest, but I'm afraid I'm going to be. It's not over.''

Parker hoped with all his might that that didn't mean that Ellie was going to march back in here next time showing a lot more skin.

Chapter Two

Ellie hid her face in her hands, wishing she could call back the last few seconds of her conversation with Parker. Had she really made that stupid comment about wearing a bikini? It wasn't even exactly what Sunny had suggested, but…

"But you were just so frustrated and angry that you couldn't be smart, could you?" Ellie asked herself, lying back on the blue floral spread of the hotel room, trying not to think of Parker Monroe's dark, silky hair or his deep amber eyes. Try as she might, she had never completely forgotten him. Most of the time, he was out of her thoughts completely, but now and then, when she would least expect it, she would dream of him, and the dream was always…erotic. His naked body poised over hers as he took her where he had taken other women so many times.

Ellie knew it was because she had once discovered Parker kissing Celia Warner silly out at Jackson Woods. It had been a rough awakening for Ellie. She had always worshipped Parker from afar, built girlish dreams about him even though she'd known his reputation, and even though he'd never shown any special interest in her beyond childhood friendship. He'd left her behind in the last couple of years he'd been home. And seeing him kissing another girl, an older girl, had been distressing. Ellie had spun away and run back home. She had done her best to erase all her foolish dreams of Parker and her fleeting memories of that kiss. And she'd done well. She was no longer a silly girl sending out longing signals to an older boy. She no longer believed in dreams or love or thought of Parker Monroe as a shining knight. Heck, she did her best not to think of the man at all.

Still, she had never completely forgotten the look of Parker's strong arms as he held Celia, or the look of intense bliss on Celia's face. At least in her subconscious. When she was awake, she was perfectly sensible and smart. But years after the fact, when Ellie lay asleep, unable to control her thoughts, now and then a vision of Parker would still come to her. Only in these restless dreams, it was not Celia Warner, but *she* who was wrapped in Parker's embrace, his mouth and body pressed to hers. She was no longer awkward, naive Ellie Donahue, a girl running from her first bruised heart, but a woman experiencing her first taste of ecstasy. And Parker was the man giving her such pleasure.

Ellie let out a groan and rubbed at her eyes, trying to obliterate the disturbing vision. No, she never had been smart where Parker was concerned, not even when she was asleep, so why should today be any different? Still, that was simply a fantasy, the kind every woman had and sometimes regretted, nothing to do with the real world. And Parker wasn't the issue here. Neither was she. The issue was Sunny and Lydia, Delia and Rosellen and even Mr. Fipps. All of Red Rose, in fact. What was she going to do about that?

She pushed her hands into her hair. ''What am I supposed to do? The darn man doesn't want to come back. We all knew that, or at least I did. You can't make a man stay when he wants to go.''

But she'd promised. She thought of Delia's tear-filled eyes, and she knew that soon, very soon, Delia would pack up and leave her home if things didn't change. There was little keeping Delia here when everything she wanted was disappearing.

Something had to change, Ellie thought. She had to make it change. And if everyone thought Parker could make a difference, then heck, she was just going to make sure he tried. Or at least that he understood just what saying no meant.

Ellie sat up in bed suddenly. She picked up the phone and began to dial. ''Sunny? I have something I want you to do for me. It might take a little work, but it's important.''

It was early evening when Parker heard the doorbell ring three times, followed by an insistent knocking, as if the person outside were being pursued by attackers.

Parker frowned. He wasn't in the mood for visitors, but he pulled open the door.

Ellie stood there, smiling up at him. It was a pasted-on smile, but a nice one nonetheless.

He smiled back. And why not? She was fully dressed. He was going to regret telling her no again, but at least he wouldn't be distracted by anything other than her eyes, the soft looking silk of her hair or those incredible legs that were more visible now that she was wearing a pair of shorts and sandals. He felt a moment of regret that he would never get to slide his fingers down those legs. But then, he didn't know why it bothered him. He'd already decided years ago that Ellie was off limits. Ellie was the most genuine girl he'd ever known. It was clear from the start that she would grow into a forever and always woman, and he wouldn't hurt or insult her by ever pretending to be that kind of man. But she did have achingly touchable legs.

Damn.

"Back so soon?" he asked, ignoring his completely inappropriate thoughts as he stepped back and gestured her inside.

"I came to Chicago just to see you. There didn't seem to be any point in waiting." She gave him a nervous smile and reached for a huge box that was sitting on the porch behind her.

"Let me help you," he said, reaching for the box, but she shook her head and held on tightly.

"Not yet. It's not that heavy. Really."

He frowned and let her by. "I may not be a gallant man, Ellie, but I'm capable of simple courtesy."

She gazed up at him with wide gray eyes, eyes that brooked no argument. Schoolteacher eyes, he used to call them. "Parker, you were stubborn, but you were never discourteous to me. So I thank you for your offer to carry this, but I don't want you to. At least not yet. And when I say no, I mean no."

He grinned. "I remember." What he also remembered was that Ellie's mother had been a good cook but was otherwise a bit of a hopeless woman who had been wronged by men, including her husband and his own father, who had apparently once propositioned her. Luann Donahue, whether she'd simply had enough or whether she was a wan creature in the first place, had left most of the child rearing for her daughters to her eldest child. Ellie had been young, but she'd learned early on how to deal with troublesome and overzealous people. She knew how to say no and get her way.

He held up his hands palm out. "The box is all yours. I wouldn't think of challenging your authority."

Her smile seemed brighter than the most expensive chandelier he owned. "Well then, we're making progress."

Parker couldn't help chuckling. "What's in the box, Ellie?" he whispered in the most coaxing way that he knew.

"I—" She blinked and shivered, as if he'd caught her off guard. "Enticement," she finally said.

Enticement. He looked down at the shining crown of her hair and knew just what the word meant. "Explain. Show me."

Ellie nodded, but she didn't hand over the box. "Parker, maybe I wasn't clear before. We don't want to force you to come home and stay. We just need your expertise for a while. We need to borrow your presence to show everyone that Red Rose is an inviting place to live."

He smiled and motioned her to a seat. "You want me to lie and pretend I come to Red Rose for pleasure?"

"It's not such a bad place." Her voice sounded hurt.

Parker instantly felt like a jerk. She was right. It wasn't Red Rose itself that had been the problem.

"It's a very nice town," he agreed. "But not for everyone. It's your town, Ellie."

"You still have property there. The house and the hotel and the building where the factory once operated."

Parker chuckled. "The hotel's been closed down for years. My father's worst business venture, worse even than the factory, it barely survived two years."

"Because people didn't come. They didn't know what Red Rose had to offer, but you could make that happen." Ellie was sitting on the sofa, her hands clutching her pretty knees as she leaned forward in her enthusiasm. "Your father wasn't really all that interested in advertising us. He wanted to keep the town as a private retreat for himself and…um, well, you know."

He knew. His father had brought his women to the hotel. Mick Monroe had always had a personal reason for doing things. Building the hotel had been no different.

"But you're not interested in keeping Red Rose for your own purposes," Ellie rushed on. "You could let people know the good things. You could save us. You know what sells and what doesn't."

She lifted her hands, and her fingers fluttered.

Parker couldn't help himself then. He sat down beside her, caught her hands in his own and turned to her. "Ellie, I counsel businesses. I don't engage in public relations. That's what you need."

"We can't afford it."

He wanted to laugh at that. If she knew what he charged his customers, she'd...well, no doubt she'd be embarrassed, and he would never want to embarrass her. It wasn't a matter of not wanting to help her. He didn't have what it took to save a town, especially a town where he had such a history.

"Look," she was saying suddenly, flipping open the lid of the box she had placed on the floor. "I've got examples, samples." She reached in and pulled out a plastic container, popped it open, and instantly the aroma of rich chocolate drifted into the room. Unable to stop himself, Parker breathed in deeply. He closed his eyes.

"Sally Mae Engels's quadruple chocolate cake. Cake made for sinners, she used to tell me."

Ellie chuckled. "Well, she just knew that you fancied yourself a sinner, and she wanted you to buy some from her shop."

"Smart lady. She stopped using the sinner line later, when I actually became one."

His voice dipped low and Ellie lowered her lashes. She ducked her head and dived back into the box. "Yes, Sally Mae knows her customers. How about this?" She brought out a small insulated bag and zipped it open. Inside was another plastic container. When she opened it, Parker knew what it was immediately.

"Orange chiffon ice cream. From Sunny's Big Babe Dairy Shop," he surmised.

"None other. She said it used to be your favorite."

It still was. He wasn't about to say that, though. "Are you trying to fatten me up, Ellie?"

She blinked and looked at him. At his body, that is. He felt his muscles tighten, felt his breath freeze in his chest. If Ellie had been a blushing woman, he would have sworn she would have been bright red. Instead, she did that thing where her lashes drooped, hiding those oh-so-revealing eyes. Ah, so Ellie knew what it was to notice a man's body? Of course, she was a woman now. Parker wished he hadn't remembered that.

''Ellie?''

She shook her head. ''Of course I'm not trying to fatten you up. Let's try this, then.''

She pulled out a long object, shrouded in plastic wrap. When she pulled back the plastic, the aroma of roses hit him. Inside lay two perfect roses, white and pink. Huge blossoms.

''From Abigail's flower shop?''

''And from Delia, who works there. You wouldn't know Delia. She's relatively new.''

''Ellie,'' he said, laying his hand on the bare skin of her arm. A bad thing to do. Touching the soft skin of her arm made him want to stroke it. Immediately he pulled back and frowned. ''Ellie, what are you trying to do?''

She ignored him and went back to her cache of goodies. In the next few minutes, she pulled out spruce boughs from Jackson Woods, wild honey and strawberries from Joyce Hives's Hives Honey and Produce and a pile of photos so thick it would take hours to go through them all.

''Here's the sunset over Eagle's Nest Hill. Remember that, Parker?''

Of course he did. He and Ellie and a big group of young people had played games there frequently when they'd been young.

"And here's the old Stone Mill. It doesn't do anything anymore, but it's pretty, don't you think?"

"Anyone would think so," he agreed, but he grabbed her hand before she could go on to the next photo. "Enough, Ellie. What are you doing? I want you to stop this and tell me. Now." Although he pretty much understood where she was heading, he wanted her to be clear, so that he could tell her it wouldn't work.

"I'm...I'm trying to seduce you," she whispered.

Parker sucked in a breath. Although he knew her meaning was innocent, and it was exactly what he'd expected, her choice of words left his ears ringing and his body throbbing.

"Seduce me?"

"Yes. Don't you see? Red Rose has so much to offer. If you could just see that, use it to bring business there, we'd be all right."

This was getting painful. He really didn't want to hurt her.

"No, Ellie—"

But she cut him off. She pulled out a folder. "Look," she told him, shuffling through the papers. "I have it all here. I had everyone fax the information. Here it is, Sunny's profit and loss statement for last year. And here's the Red Rose Boutique, the drug store, the gas station, Chesney's Floral, all the rest. Here we are, Parker, our lives, our failings. I've tried to show you the best of Red Rose. Here's the worst. This is our future if something doesn't change. Don't you care about Sally Mae and Sunny and Abigail and the others? Do you want me to beg?"

Her voice broke slightly, and he cursed himself for bringing her to this.

"Don't do this, Ellie. Don't...don't try so hard." He'd told her that once before, he remembered, when she'd been very young and sobbing over a C on a math test.

"I don't know how to be any other way," she said, and her voice was clear and honest, and besides, he knew that it was true. Ellie was a straight-shooter, she was a doer, a caretaker, a have-to-try kind of person. It was why the town had sent her.

"I'll go down on my knees if that's what you need, Parker. Just don't send me back to break their hearts and doom our home."

For a moment he thought she was going to drop to her knees right before him. For a moment, hot male need rose up in him and he wanted her to. And then self-hatred took its place. What kind of man had he become? He'd said that he was worse than his father. Well, he hadn't known just how much worse if he could take Ellie's innocent plea and turn it into a sexual fantasy.

He grasped her chin roughly. "Don't do it." He forced the words from between clenched teeth. "Don't even think of begging me."

She started to open her mouth. He kissed her. Roughly. A warning. To her and to himself.

"Don't say another word," he said, his voice as clipped and harsh as his kiss had been.

She opened her eyes wide and touched her lips as if he'd hurt her somehow. Maybe he had.

Parker closed his eyes. He walked a few steps away. But when he turned and looked at her, all he could see was the red of her mouth where his kiss had punished her, the wounded look in her eyes and that stubborn tilt of her chin that told him that despite his abuse, she was going to try again.

He drew in a breath and shook his head, holding his hand out to stop her from speaking.

"All right, I'll come." His voice was low and resigned and hard. "You win. You've got me. I'll come now if you want. Might as well get this over with. Just let me make a few calls. I'll try to help. But it won't save Red Rose. Some things are just impossible. And I can't stay long."

She nodded, one quick sharp move. "Give us three weeks. A start. That's all I want from you."

He wondered if her words were a warning, but he was past caring.

He was returning to Red Rose. Ellie Parker didn't just know how to say no. She knew how to get a man to say yes.

Ellie glanced across at Parker from her seat on the passenger side of his red Jaguar. He'd insisted on having Jeb drive her little subcompact back to Red Rose while she rode with him.

"You'll need to fill me in if I'm going to do anything," he'd explained, but she wasn't convinced that that was the real reason she was now securely strapped into his car. He'd had only one look at her twelve-year-old car which listed slightly and which had a dented fender and had decided instantaneously that her transportation wasn't reliable or safe, which just wasn't true.

"This is a sports car. It's no safer than mine," she said stubbornly.

Parker turned his wicked grin on her. "In the right hands, this car is safety personified."

His voice was low and seductive, and Ellie had to swallow hard. She also had to admit that he was an expert behind the wheel. No surprise. The Monroes had always excelled in physical pursuits.

And that was just something that didn't bear thinking of. She'd be much better off trying to decide what she was going to do with Parker when she got him home. His father's old hotel was an abandoned pit, and the Monroe homestead had been deserted for years. She'd called ahead and asked Sunny to break in and do something about the place, but it was clear that there wouldn't be time to accomplish much in the mere two-and-a-half hours they had.

Over two hours later she was still thinking furiously, plotting a rocky path, hoping that bringing Parker back was the right thing to do.

"What are you thinking?" he asked. "We're almost there, but you don't look relieved. You look worried."

She was. "I'm not. I'm just planning." Which was true.

"What are you planning?"

"You need a place to sleep." The words just popped right out of her mouth.

He raised a brow. "You didn't anticipate that I'd actually come with you?"

She raised one shoulder. "We hoped, but the ladies tend to be a bit superstitious. Setting up a place to house you would have been considered a jinx."

He chuckled. "I can sleep anywhere. Under any conditions."

"That's good, then. Sunny most likely had to break a window to get into your house, and she'll probably be able to provide a decent mattress, but beyond that

I can't promise anything. We need a few days to fix you up properly."

"You don't have to do that, Ellie."

"We do. We will. We want you to feel welcome." And on that thought, she realized that he was headed toward the east side of town, the part where the abandoned shoe factory was the first thing that met the eye, and the giant hideous statue that the town had erected was the next thing. "No, let's go in from the west," she said. "Turn here and circle around."

No doubt he knew what she was doing, but she didn't care. The west side of town had been planted with roses and shrubs. It was the good side, a sign of promise.

"It's okay, Ellie," Parker said softly. "I know what to expect."

"The west side," she insisted, and he picked up her hand and kissed it.

"Yes, my imperious lady," he whispered.

A long shiver went through Ellie. Her breasts felt tight. She felt the need to cross her legs, but knew that he would notice. He was teasing her, and couldn't possibly know how much even his voice affected her, but if she showed any reaction, he might notice.

"You're a good servant," she teased, trying to keep her voice calm.

"Of course." It was a game he'd obliged her by playing when they were young and she was still fanciful. "To the west side."

Ellie sat back, confident that in this one moment at least, Red Rose would look its best.

Parker made the turn. He pointed the car toward the roses and shrubs and the big Welcome to Red

Rose that they'd erected last year in a vain hope that it would bring in visitors.

And then she saw something. Beneath the sign, sleeping in the fading sunlight was Mr. Fipps. He'd gotten into the habit lately. He was harmless enough, so most of the time no one cared.

But eleven years ago, she remembered, Mr. Fipps had been the most vociferous of those accusing Parker of impregnating Mitzi. He'd yelled louder even than Uncle Cliff. He'd said vile things to Parker, irrevocable things.

She glanced across to Parker.

Don't notice, she thought. Please don't notice. But the sight of a sleeping man curled up beneath the sign was impossible to ignore. Parker rolled the car to a stop.

He stared down at the man who had yelled ugly hateful things at him the night he'd left.

''Welcome to Red Rose,'' Parker read, his voice a monotone.

''Yes, welcome to Red Rose,'' she whispered fiercely, and ignoring the fact that touching Parker was forbidden, ignoring the pounding of her heart that told her she was tempting the lion, she reached over and threaded her fingers through Parker Monroe's.

He was home for now. She would try her best to keep him here for a while.

Chapter Three

Ellie was pouring coffee the next morning at the Red Rose Café when Parker walked through the door. He glanced around at the women who were gathered there, waiting for the business day to begin.

"Morning, ladies," he said, his voice deep and low as he turned his gaze on Ellie.

"That's so nice," Sunny said. "A real man's voice in our midst. Almost makes a woman want to cry...or do something wicked."

But Ellie didn't feel as if she wanted to cry. Parker was staring at her with a frown on his face. She knew why, and she wanted to run.

"You promised to wake me," he told her.

She had, but then when she'd gotten up this morning, she'd realized he had no phone. Her knock hadn't had any effect, and when she'd gone next door, circled the house and peered in his bedroom window, she'd seen him, lying there, sleeping. Only a small triangle of sheet covered his hips. In fact, she wasn't sure it had completely covered him at all, since she'd hastily glanced away. There had been no way she was going to rap on his window and wake him up, knowing that when she did that bit of sheet would slip away completely.

"I thought you deserved to sleep in on your first day," she lied. My, she was beginning to pick up bad habits.

"The sooner we get started, the sooner we'll finish."

"Oh Ellie, a man of purpose. I'd forgotten just how direct the Monroe men are," Lydia drawled. "Pour the man a cup of coffee, Ellie."

"Sit here, Parker," Delia said. "You don't know me yet, but I'm ever so grateful."

"We're so glad you agreed to come help us, Parker," Joyce said in her soft lilt.

"Yes, so grateful," another feminine voice whispered.

Ellie looked around. There were only a few feet between herself and Parker, but those few feet were crammed with women, and it was clear that Parker held their attention completely. She could have poured the coffee on her head and it was doubtful that anyone would notice. The estrogen was flowing strong, more like gushing. Not for the first time she noticed that a number of Sunday dresses had come out this morning. There was more perfume in the air, more earrings, more makeup.

Red Rose had come alive this morning.

She grinned at Parker. "Yes, have a seat, Parker. Have some coffee."

"All right then, I will," he said in a low drawl. "If you sit first." He reached over and grabbed a chair, placing it right behind her. His hands were only inches behind her bottom. She could feel his warmth and his presence just like a caress. The urge to lean back and actually experience his touch was almost overpowering, and for a moment Ellie couldn't help thinking that Parker Monroe was a lot more potent than he had been eleven years ago. He had certainly developed whatever it was that his father had possessed, that incredible something that made women abandon their husbands just for the thrill of one night in his bed.

"Sit," he said again, and this time his lips were just behind her ear.

She spilled the coffee all over the table.

The spell broken, she reached for a cloth and scrubbed at the table. "I have to work," she said, hoping her voice didn't sound too breathless.

"You worked yesterday. You came to Chicago. You delivered me just as you said you would." He took the cloth and the coffeepot from her and gave her a gentle push, propelling her back onto the chair. Then he signaled Lydia, who brought him a fresh pot of coffee and a new cloth. He held the cloth out of Ellie's reach, wiped up the spill and poured her coffee.

He sat down and looked around the room.

The women gathered there were positively glowing.

"On behalf of all of us here, I thank you," Lydia said. "You are just what we need to shake things up."

"We'll see," Parker said, noncommittally, but he gave Lydia a fond look.

"You're a blessing, Parker," one woman said. "Just a blessing. A saint."

Ellie almost felt Parker stiffen in her seat. This wouldn't do. She'd barely managed to get the man here. This kind of talk would only have the wrong effect.

"Parker's going to try to help us," she said firmly. "That's all we can ask of anyone."

"Oh no. Now that I see him, I can tell you're wrong. He's the one. He's going to save our town, aren't you, Mr. Monroe?" one young woman barely out of high school asked. Ellie looked at the girl's wide, worshipful eyes. She thought she heard Parker mutter "hell" underneath his breath.

"Let's get out of here," he said, tossing money on the table and tugging on Ellie's hand.

"You just got here," one woman protested.

"Where are you taking Ellie?" another asked.

Parker grinned. "Back to my bed to have my way with her, Mrs. Murphy. That's what us Monroe men do best, you know." And he leaned down and gave Mrs. Murphy, an aging widow, a kiss on the cheek.

The woman shrieked and blushed, but she held her hand close against the spot where his lips had touched her as if she were savoring a precious gift.

"Oh, I like this one. He's full of the devil. Just what we need," she declared.

"Nice touch," Ellie said dryly as they exited the building. "You didn't need to make them think that we were heading off for a few hours of sin." There were those who still believed that he'd had his way with Mitzi and with other girls years ago, and they were no doubt partially right. Parker hadn't been a saint or even close, but Ellie didn't want to think about that. She knew she sounded like a prude, but she couldn't seem to help herself.

"Ellie, have I embarrassed you? I have, haven't I?"

He hadn't embarrassed her. He'd reminded her of who and what he was. "I just think you should be trying to shed your reputation, not enhance it."

"Do you really think that's what they want?" He motioned back toward the Red Rose Café.

She sighed. "No, you're right. They want the excitement, the adventure. They just want to feel alive, I guess, and you gave them that."

"That won't save your town, however."

"No, it will just make them forget their troubles for a while. Come on. Since we're out, I might as well take you on a tour of the town. We need to do that anyway. We need to get started. Then you can decide what our next step should be."

"As if I know."

"Well, none of us do. It won't hurt to let someone else have a whack at things. Maybe gain some fresh perspective."

But a short time later, she wasn't so sure. She had lived in this town all her life, she loved Red Rose, but now, looking at it through the eyes of someone who had not loved it, who had run from it, Ellie felt defensive.

The buildings in town were clean and neat enough, but there weren't all that many. The streets were wide, but somewhat empty. And out on the highway, leading to some of the other sights, she felt a moment of panic as they neared the part of the tour she'd been dreading.

Parker saw the monstrosity before she pulled into the lot.

"Well, that's...intriguing," he managed to say. And he did appear to be intrigued. There, sitting right next to Sunny's Big Babe Dairy Shop was a woman the size of an oak tree with breasts as big as tractor tires. She had a red, painted-on dress that left little to the imagination. "I take it she's Big Babe?"

Ellie managed to give a curt nod. "Yes, there was a time, just over a year ago, when we decided we needed some landmarks. The plan was to have each owner erect a statue personifying the business. The only trouble was that after Big Babe went up, everyone else backed out. Lydia let this statue stand, but she said that she wanted Red Rose to look inviting, not like a B movie set. Still Sunny likes Babe, and we are right on the edge of town, so Lydia and the town council gave her a pass."

Parker looked down at Ellie. "Ellie, you're squirming."

"I'm not." But she was.

"Babe isn't so bad."

"She looks, um...a bit like a prostitute."

"You'd know that, would you? Lots of prostitutes in Red Rose these days?" He was smiling so knowingly that she had half a mind to say yes.

"Of course not, but you know what I mean. Her skirt is doing that Marilyn Monroe thing and she has these huge...parts."

"Really? I hadn't noticed."

Which was a great big fat lie, since he was clearly teasing her.

"Anyway, now you've seen all of Red Rose there is to see," Ellie said, starting to turn the car around.

Which wasn't quite true. From their position on the road, the abandoned shoe factory was in sight, and beyond that, one more structure could be seen in the distance. Three stories tall, its pink paint peeling badly, the Honeymoon Suites from Heaven Hotel sat there, a monument to Mick Monroe's own descent into narcissism. He'd thought he could do anything, make anything pay and that he could play any kind of game and win. He'd thought he could hurt people and no one would notice. He'd been wrong. The shoe factory had been proof that Mick had been human and fallible, but the hotel had been a blaring banner that trumpeted the man's misplaced arrogance and decadence. Ellie saw Parker take one look at the building, then turn his head away.

She hadn't wanted to bring up that part of his past, but some things just couldn't stay hidden. Like big pink hotels and bad memories. She knew that as well as he did.

Sporting a smile and hoping she could take his mind off those bad memories, Ellie turned around and drove back the way they'd come, searching for a change of topic. "So...what do you think of our, um...unique situation, big-bosomed statues and all, Mr. Consultant?" she finally asked.

She turned her head to look at Parker and found that he was already staring at her with those deep amber eyes. "I think that Red Rose is a quaint little town, but its time has come and gone," he said, not wasting words.

Her smile turned into a frown. "No."

"Ellie, nothing lasts forever."

"Things can last forever. Maybe not in the same format, but Red Rose can survive."

"And if it changes, will you still love it? Will it still be right for you?"

"What do you mean?"

He motioned for her to pull over to the side of the road. He exited the car and circled around to help her out. Then he turned her to face the heart of the town, still more than a block away.

"Look at it Ellie. There's Red Rose, all pink and white and clean. You have the necessities of a drugstore and a gas station, but then there's the honey shop, the beauty shop, the flower shop, the boutique and the café, all done up in frills and bows and flowers. This is a woman's town, Ellie. Here you call the shots. All the shots, all the time. That wasn't always the case. Do you really want to change that?"

She knew what he meant. She'd wondered the same things herself. In truth, she didn't really know, but she knew what everyone else wanted. Or maybe the word wasn't wanted, but needed. Red Rose was a woman's town, and there were many good things about it, but it had become a sad town on a downhill run.

"We have to change things. We need more if we're to go on beyond this generation."

"You're sure?"

"Yes. I...I want change," she said, her voice a bit wobbly. "How can we do it? What would bring men to Red Rose, Parker? I don't really know that much about what men want, and it seems that no one else does, either. We've tried to bring men in, but we don't seem to be hitting it right."

Parker gazed down into Ellie's face, so worried and serious. He hated the fact that she was facing the loss of everything she loved, no matter what happened. If the town changed, it wouldn't be the same town that had cradled her all her life. If it didn't change, she might not have a home. The terrible thing was that he didn't have a clue how to help her. There was nothing about this town that would entice a company to pull up roots and settle here. No major waterway, no city, no easy source of cheap labor.

But he wasn't ready to admit that to Ellie yet. Gazing down at her, what Parker really thought was that she needed some life in her life, some fun for a change.

''What do men want?'' he asked. ''Well, Big Babe was a good shot.''

She rolled her eyes and shook her head at him the way she had when they were kids and he had said something outrageous or unbelievable. ''Honestly,'' she said. ''You see. I just don't get the whole 'man' thing. What's so great about belching or spitting or sex or taking things apart and not being able to get them back together?''

But Parker's mind stopped cold on the sex part. That one statement was enough to let him know that she'd never been made love to properly.

His gaze went instantly to her lips and he noted they were pink and full and utterly kissable. Had she missed out on the best part of touching because there were simply not enough men around here to get the job done right? Well then, that was a crime. Ellie should have known the pleasures of touching, the thrill of having a man's flesh against her own as he tasted her, savored her, lost himself in her.

''Parker?''

Parker blinked. He stared down at Ellie and saw

that her eyes were wide and worried, her lips parted slightly.

"Damn Red Rose," he whispered.

"What?" She swallowed hard.

"You should be married," he said. "You should have babies. If I help you, that'll happen. Getting husbands and babies for all of you...that's what this is all about, anyway, isn't it?"

She shook her head vehemently. "Not for me. I don't want a husband. Or babies, either. I've had some bad experiences with men and...don't you remember my father?"

He did. The man had been a selfish jerk, a taker who had dedicated his life to impregnating his wife and not much else. He'd gotten drunk on the night his youngest was born and driven his truck into a gulley, ending his life and the endless run of Donahue babies. Ellie's mother had been lost, burying herself in her work cooking for the Monroes, and as a result, Ellie had had more of raising babies by thirteen than most women had experienced by thirty.

Parker couldn't help noticing that Ellie didn't mention his own father who had been even worse than hers, but he was sure that Mick Monroe had contributed to Ellie's statement that she didn't want a husband. He wondered who the other men had been who had given her a distaste for marriage and felt a sudden urge to sock some unknown guy in the eye. Still, there *were* good men out there. He was sure of that much. If enough men came to Red Rose, some of them would be the right kind. And maybe men like Mick Monroe, Zach Donahue and himself would be forgotten in time. Maybe the past could go away if something good came in to replace it. But that wasn't the point right now. Ellie and her ladies were the point.

"So…this isn't about husbands?"

"It is, just not about mine. I'd like to see my friends and maybe even some of my sisters happily married, if there is such a thing. Do you—"

He looked down at her expectantly.

"Do you think there is such a thing as a happy marriage?" she asked.

"For some. Not for me. I love women, but for me there's only friendship, there's only…"

"Sex?" she asked, wide-eyed.

Parker couldn't help grinning. She was trying to be so frank, yet she was so clearly uncomfortable just saying the word.

"Well, not always sex," he whispered, leaning close. "Sometimes there's just friendship, or kissing, or sometimes friendship and kissing."

And if she hadn't been Ellie, if he hadn't promised himself years ago never to go near her in the most basic sense, he might have demonstrated. Instead, he looked for a change of subject.

"So what exactly *do* you want me to do for Red Rose?" he asked. "Specifically."

Her eyes lit up, but her hands fluttered. "I'm not sure, specifically. We just need something that will bring in men," Ellie insisted.

"We need an orderly plan," he agreed. "When I counsel a business, I always suggest that we start with a list of what we have and what we want. In this case, since we're shooting blindly into the dark, I'd suggest an open house, a party of sorts touting all that's best in Red Rose. It's going to take a lot of work and a fair amount of time. If we're very lucky, we might get a few nibbles, someone who might see some potential here and agree to give the town a try.''

''An open house? That's wonderful.''

It was a great big shot in the dark, but hearing the enthusiasm in her voice, seeing the worry fade was enough to compel him to stay and see it through.

''Do you think it will bring in a lot of people?''

''Too soon to tell. All we can do is our homework.'' And hope, he thought.

''I always do my homework, Parker. Now…where are we going to put all those people when they arrive in town? We need some place big and empty, with lots of rooms.''

She looked at him pointedly.

''No,'' he said. ''Absolutely not.''

''It's the only place that has enough room.''

''Much of it is little better than a bordello, Ellie, and a crumbling one at that. At least one of the rooms is wall-to-wall bed.''

''I'd heard that, but I never really knew it was true. Maybe that's a good thing, though.''

''Excuse me?''

''Well, I saw the way you looked at Big Babe. Most of us except Sunny are a bit embarrassed by her, but you weren't. You thought she was fun. Maybe if we change the name of the hotel and clean it up, they won't mind the cathouse decor all that much. Maybe they wouldn't even notice.''

Parker couldn't help laughing now. ''Ellie, slow down. I said I'd try to help you a little. Opening the hotel is a completely different matter.''

''But it would be the right thing to do. You left town in a cloud. Wouldn't it be great if you came back and saved the hotel and saved us, too?''

"I've told you that isn't going to happen. I don't know a thing about saving people and wouldn't want to try. Why do you keep saying that?"

"I don't know. Maybe because I saw what happened in the Red Rose Café today. Things were different, just because you were there. I like that. I like helping my friends that way. Friends help friends. You were my friend once, weren't you?"

He looked at her. She was a woman now, but he still saw the eager little girl trying to raise her family almost on her own. So earnest, so fervent, so determined to stand up to life and take what she could get for those she loved.

She had been a danger to his peace of mind even then.

Now, in the full bloom of womanhood and desirability, she was many times more dangerous. Because no, he couldn't stay. Not like the men that Red Rose wanted to tempt.

"Parker?"

He took a deep breath. He thought of that monstrosity of a hotel sitting on the edge of town, of this town that was fading like colored paper left out in the sun too long. He thought of all his successes which had been elsewhere, and his failures which had been here. Then he looked down at Ellie again, Ellie who had come to Chicago and dared him to try where he had failed.

If he could just bring her one good man who would stay, he would be free of this town forever. He could have peace.

He tucked his finger beneath her chin and tipped her head back. "We're friends. I'll try," he said.

''Just remember who and what I am, a man who never did follow the rules.''

And then he kissed her, breaking the rule he'd laid down years ago on the day he had realized that he was a danger to Ellie.

But now this was different. He needed to let her know that he was a Monroe through and through, and so he touched her with his tongue. Slowly, deliberately, stroking her. She let him. She shivered slightly, rising on her toes, and then when he pulled away, she crossed her arms and glanced at him.

''You can't scare me off that easily, Parker. I know your game.''

Somehow he gathered his wits about him and controlled his own reaction to touching her. Heat had exploded within him, and he'd wanted to touch more of her. He couldn't think of that right now.

He managed to smile and shake his head. ''That's good then, Ellie. That makes one of us, because I don't know my game, and I don't know what in hell I'm doing here.''

''You're here to lure the men in,'' she said simply. ''Let's get started. Now what should we use to catch them?''

Chapter Four

All right, the hotel was a monstrosity, Ellie admitted, a few minutes later, after she'd dragged Parker over to tour the place. It had sat there for years, big and pink and empty, and she hardly ever thought of it at all. In fact, it was such a part of the day-to-day landscape that she barely even noticed it. But up close, now that she was taking an interest in its future, things were different. The sign, which still read Honeymoon Suites from Heaven, was painted gold, which had mostly peeled away, leaving it pocked and spotted. The bright pink brick was garish and the flat roof was sagging at the corners.

"Okay, it's not very promising," she conceded, "but it's all we've got for now. With a little paint and some basic carpentry, it would pass. A bit of water and elbow grease could work wonders, too. And maybe different curtains. Those in the windows look sad and old, but I can run those up on the machine in no time. Lace, I think. It wouldn't take much work or money.'' Her voice picked up speed as she spoke. And then she realized that she was doing all the talking. She was letting her thoughts get in front of her good sense. Ellie froze. Her face felt warm, and she turned her gaze on Parker, giving a hesitant shrug. ''That is...we could do all that if you agree to it.''

She gave Parker an uncertain look. His arms were crossed. He was grinning.

''You always were one to take hold of a project and run with it, weren't you, Ellie?''

Her face felt even warmer. She could remember several such times when they were children when she had tackled idiotic dreams, trying to make them somehow practical by planning all the details.

''I'm old enough now to realize that I can't have everything the way I want it to be,'' she argued. ''This *is* your hotel.''

He shook his head. ''No, it's not. It was my father's, and it's mine only because he willed it to me. But you're right about the hotel. I hate this place, but if we're going to invite people to come to an open house, we have to put them somewhere. I'm the one who suggested an open house, and I don't do things by half measures, at least where business is concerned. If we're going to try and bring the world to Red Rose, we're going to do it right. Let's go see what kind of damage we'll have to repair in the interior.''

''Do you have a key?''

He smiled and reached behind a flowerpot, pulling out a dirt-encrusted key.

Ellie blinked. ''That's been there all this time?''

''Some things never change, Ellie.'' His voice was slightly hoarse and tired. She had the feeling that he was referring to himself rather than the habit of leaving the key where anyone could find it. The thought scared her to death. She'd been half in love with him when he was a boy. If he hadn't changed…

She slammed the door on that thought. *She* had changed.

"Some things never change," she agreed, "but some things do." She swept her hand out in an arc that encompassed the decaying building. "Let's hope it hasn't changed too much inside."

Parker coughed and looked mildly frazzled as he shoved the key into the lock. "Let's hope it has."

Ellie felt warmth climbing her throat. Of course, she'd heard that the inside of the hotel was a bit suggestive. Still, when she stepped inside, she saw nothing terribly wrong. The gold carpeting was thick with dust, and the heavy maroon couches were not only dusty but deep and long enough to sleep on. Still, the room was actually rather sterile. No other furnishings filled the spaces. No pictures graced the walls. There was, in fact, not a hint of the decadence people had whispered about all her life.

Ellie blinked. "It's…different from what I expected."

Parker chuckled, a humorless sound. "That was the idea, to make the public view look very ordinary, lest some poor clueless soul should wander in accidentally. And dear old dad even kept a room or two for the unsuspecting innocent, but the majority of the rooms were tailored to the more carnal visitor. Not a very lucrative business move, since Red Rose is such a small town. No man of our parents' generation wanted the whole world to know that he was taking his wife out for a night of intense sexual play, and certainly no man wanted anyone to know he was taking someone here who wasn't his wife. At least, except for Mick Monroe. Consequently, most of Dad's guests came from out of town, and not many of them wanted to travel all the way to Red Rose in search of a bed and a woman.

"Most of the men were here at one time or another just to look, but very few of them ever slept behind these walls."

His voice was clipped. Ellie wondered just how many times Mick Monroe had humiliated his family. But maybe the number didn't matter. He had done it, and done it knowingly. This hotel must be like a slap in the face for Parker.

"New carpeting could be expensive," she said, "but if you wouldn't mind, we could change things, make it a place so different from the original that no one would ever know."

"Ellie," Parker said. "Everyone knows. This is small-town America."

He was right. People here had long memories.

"Well then," she said, hands on her hips. "We won't pretend it didn't happen. We'll make the place look respectable, but before we do, we'll take a few pictures. Tasteful black-and-whites, artsy shots, the kind they have in museums to depict the past. Patsy Krandon can do it. And then, when we redecorate, we'll post some of the photos and the notorious history on the walls, the way they do sometimes in historic buildings. Kind of a museumlike touch. That way all those people who were too embarrassed to come here but were still curious can have a vicarious experience reliving the past of the Honeymoon Suites from Heaven."

He studied her for several seconds, those golden eyes hot and speculative. Ellie had an urge to look down and make sure that her clothes were still on. She felt naked, pinned.

"You know, that's a very good idea," he finally said. "If we have to reopen this behemoth, then let's do it with some style."

But still he continued to stare.

"What...what are you looking at?" she asked, forcing herself to raise her chin and pretend indifference. "Do I have a coffee stain on my shirt?"

Wrong question. His eyes dropped to her chest. Heat zipped through her. She was thankful that the padding in her bra hid her budding nipples from view. Still, she started to lift her arms to cover herself, catching herself dead in the act. Too late. The sudden grin on Parker's face told her that he hadn't missed that move.

"I'm no better than my father, Ellie, but I don't mess around with the Donahue girls. Never did. Never will. I like you too much. You're safe, honey."

She carefully moved her arms so that they hung loose at her sides. She tilted her chin higher. "I knew that, Parker." And just because she didn't like the way her heart was fluttering, she forced herself to smile seductively. "But how do you know that *you're* safe? We haven't had much in the way of men here for some time."

Ah, that brought his eyebrows winging upwards. "Are you coming on to me, Ellie?" He took a step forward.

She wanted to lean forward and so she scooted back. "No, I'm just warning you. If you keep talking about how much you're like your daddy and how many women you've slept with, there are going to be women in this town who won't leave you alone. You need to decide if that's what you want.''

He nodded. ''I respect the women of this town. I won't stay, and so I won't kiss and run, either. I'll be as celibate as a rock, Ellie. No need to worry about me.''

''I wasn't.'' Which was a total lie. Every time he said his father's name, she worried. She'd known some of what Mick Monroe was. She'd had a jerk of a father herself. Those things affected a person, sometimes for a lifetime.

And Parker's comments about his father made her realize a part of why he'd left and why he could never be comfortable here. The fact that she'd been a part of coaxing him back didn't sit well with her. She'd been his friend once.

''We'll try not to entangle you too much in our affairs,'' she promised.

He shrugged. ''I came of my own free will, Ellie,'' he said, his voice low and shivery. ''I'm a grown man now, and you're a grown woman. It's true that I don't like being here, and I especially don't like this hotel, but the past can't hurt us, even if remembering it is unpleasant. I intend to help the ladies here, and that was a very good idea of how to mix the hotel's past and present. The women of Red Rose are lucky to have you on board.''

''I'm a part of this town, and I always will be,'' she said. It was a reminder, to her, to him. They came from a shared past, but their futures would follow different roads. She needed to remember that, to never let herself forget it. If she ever did, she might end up like one of Mick Monroe's women, just a ghost in a musty old building with too many regrets.

"Let's go see the rest," she said.

He sighed and then chuckled. "You're not going to like it."

"I don't like a lot of things I've faced over the years, but I know how to deal with unpleasantness."

"All right then, just one room for starters."

He led the way into the bowels of the hotel.

It was worse than he remembered, Parker thought as he gave in to Ellie's wishes to see more and opened one room after another. He and Ellie peered inside each one. His father had obviously put a lot of thought into this place. Every bed was different: circles, squares, hearts, mattresses that vibrated or ones that had mattresses that looked like rolling waves. Abstract paintings of lush naked women and lusty men graced the walls.

He turned around to see that Ellie's eyes were deliciously wide.

"All right, you get the idea," he said after the fifth room.

She nodded. "But I didn't come just to see what it was like, Parker. I need to know what needs doing if we're going to use past history as a selling point. That means getting the whole picture."

He thought about her idea, which had seemed good at the time.

"Um...Ellie?"

"Yes?" She looked up at him, wide-eyed, innocently lovely in the midst of this former flesh haven, and he wanted to groan.

"Maybe we should just bulldoze this place."

She frowned. ''We don't have time to build a new hotel, Parker.''

He sighed. She was right.

''Just show me some more,'' she coaxed, and he opened the next door.

Bad mistake. A dusty, yellowed copy of the Kama Sutra lay open on the bed, as if inviting visitors to flip through the pages. The sculpture on the bedside table was expensive, a collector's item, a fertility symbol shaped like a man who had better than average chances of getting a date if anatomy had anything to do with it. Several other similar items were scattered throughout the room. Unlike the other rooms, which had been done up in pastels and had played to more veiled and sometimes even more romantic fantasies, this one was raw, blatantly suggestive, his father's hand evident everywhere. He moved to shut the door, but Ellie pushed past him.

''Look at that,'' she said, her voice hushed.

He frowned and turned to see what she was looking at.

''Isn't that beautiful?'' she asked.

He opened his eyes wide when he realized what she was referring to. On the wall opposite the door, a long robe hung on a satin hanger. All crimson with cream-colored lapels, it was heavily embroidered with rich tribal scenes: a man approaching a tribal chieftain, laden with gifts and animals, beseeching the hand of a woman; another scene of him leading the woman back to his hut, bereft of all his possessions; and another scene of the man laying the woman down and covering her with his body as the moon and stars passed overhead. His father had obviously placed it here because of the subject matter, but Ellie moved closer and touched one finger to the bright threads that coursed through the material.

"Someone spent a lot of time on this. In spite of its setting, you can see that it was handcrafted, made with love and good intentions. This has got to go in your museum," she declared. "It's a treasure." And her smile lit up the room, as if she had never realized that anyone could ever have bad intentions. Parker knew that wasn't true. She had done her share of suffering and paying for other's injustices.

"Done," he said. "Now, Ellie, can we leave this? Let me take you home. The clock's ticking."

Immediately she raised her head, a guilty look on her face. "Oh, of course, there's work to be done. That's...that's why you're here. Let's go." And immediately she was the serious little woman again, the woman who had driven to Chicago to bring him back here to save her town.

Funny. For a moment he had imagined her naked except for a crimson-and-cream robe sliding from her shoulders, her smile welcoming as she lay back and reached up for him.

Parker shook his head. He waited for Ellie to precede him from the room, then closed it with a click.

Back at her house, he started to walk her to her door. She peered over her shoulder toward his house. "Did Sunny tell you that she was going to come over and clean your house today?" she asked.

"She did. I told her that she didn't have to do that. I would hire someone."

Ellie chuckled. "So...did she slug you or just spit in your eye?"

"Neither," Parker said with a smile. "She offered

to arm wrestle me. If I lost, she got to clean the place. If I won, I could bring in my outsider women.''

''Did you win?''

He grinned. ''Do you think I don't know better than to buck Sunny when she sneers and uses the term 'outsider women'? Her point was clear. I'm here to bring men to the town, not more women. I left the door open so she could get in.''

Ellie smiled. ''Let's go see if she made any headway on the dust. Your house has been locked up for a long time.''

And she charged ahead, not waiting for him to say yes. Clearly Ellie had gotten used to being a woman in command in the years since he'd been gone. He wondered how she'd respond to a man who wanted to conquer her.

If he brought men into the town, there would be some who would want to do just that.

Which was none of his business, of course, so Parker turned and followed her up the two wooden stairs to his porch and into his house.

''Well, I guess they don't call her Sunny for nothing,'' he remarked when Ellie spun around, examining the change in the room. ''How did she do so much so fast?''

Ellie tilted her head. ''Our Sunny is a determined woman. She prides herself on being able to do the work of ten. And then again, she probably knew just where everything should be and what she wanted to do. She used to sub for your mother's cleaning lady now and then when the woman was sick. Remember?''

He did. Sunny had been a married woman back in

those days and she had picked up odd jobs now and then to help support her and her husband.

''She ever hear from Delwyn?'' Sunny's husband had left town with another woman just when Sunny had decided that she wanted to have children.

''Yes, he called once about seven years ago. He begged her to take him back and told her that she was a woman who needed a man. She told him that yes, he was right, but he wasn't a man or anything even close to it.''

''I can almost hear her saying it. Good for her. My mother always liked Sunny. So did I.''

''Your mother, is she well?''

''Last time I talked to her, she was fine.'' His voice came out edgier than he intended. Because he and his mother didn't talk often. Since his father's death and his mother's eventual remarriage, they had grown a bit closer, but she was always going to look at him and see Mick Monroe. She'd made that clear years ago, and that just didn't make for an easy relationship.

Parker realized that his anger must have been evident in his words, because when he looked at Ellie, she was twisting her fingers.

''I'm sorry. I shouldn't have asked,'' she said softly. ''I know the two of you didn't part on good terms. I should have remembered and kept my mouth shut, but I never was very good at minding my own business, was I?''

There she was, beating up on herself, criticizing herself the way he'd heard her father criticize her when he was drunk. Parker had hated that man for doing that to her and her sisters. And so it was just natural that he had to reach out and grasp her chin.

It wouldn't have been right to let her think that he was in any way critical of her.

"Ellie," he said gently, and he felt her tremble beneath his fingertips. "Ask anything you want of me. We were neighbors, remember? You knew my family. You and I were friends once."

And then they hadn't been such close friends anymore. He didn't say that, though, because he was the one who had stopped it. He remembered the day so clearly when Ellie's cousin, Mitzi, had told him that a teenaged Ellie had a crush on him. He couldn't even begin to express to himself how that had scared him. It had cut deep and he'd wanted to save her, to ask her if she didn't know that she was asking for trouble mooning after a Monroe male?

But he figured she *did* know, a little. She was so very young, and plucking at danger, daring to risk your soul was a part of being young.

"It's enough to know that she's well," she said, shrugging as she walked around and gazed at the room that she'd seldom been allowed to enter when she was a child.

Of course, Ellie had never really been a child. She'd seemed old even when she was very young. And the problem with finding out that Ellie had wanted to have her first taste of danger with him, was that he couldn't let her do it. He'd grown up knowing that the Donahues were special. Their very poverty and the fact that they depended on his family for work made them special, his family's responsibility even if he hadn't been friends with Ellie. The fact that he had been, only made him even more aware of how important it was that he never take advantage of any of the Donahue girls. Especially after his father had tried to take advantage of Ellie's mother.

His friendship with Ellie had been one of the few areas of his life where the stigma of Mick Monroe never came into play. It had been completely innocent and free. So, he'd been sad to find out that Mick had intruded, sadder still to realize that Ellie thought of him that way. And he'd been angry as well, because it meant that he had to stay away from her. His very anger had made him consider saying something cruel to Ellie to push her away, but she'd looked up at him with those big, solemn, gray eyes, and he'd been unable to do more than walk away. In the end, that was what he'd done. He'd walked away time after time. He'd done his best to steer clear of her. Then he'd left town without saying goodbye.

And now he was back, temporarily, and Ellie was pacing his living room, her life force drawing him again, even though things hadn't changed all that much.

He was the same old Parker, a loner, a man who couldn't stay with one person for very long without wanting to be gone, just as his father had been. And Ellie was still the kind who stayed in one place and would stay with one person forever.

When she found that one person.

Parker ignored the raw wound feeling that thought gave him. He would never belong here, didn't want to. And he wanted to stop these uncomfortable musings right now. For years now, he hadn't felt this way. He didn't like feeling this way. If Ellie would go, he could get hold of himself and get down to business, get out of here fast.

"Looks good. Looks livable," he said, indicating

the room. "I can work here just fine." He pointed his stare her way, forced himself to frown, to look impatient.

She blinked and crossed her arms over her elbows, drawing into herself.

"Well then, that's good. I'll just be getting home," she said. "Lots to do."

Parker nodded, meaning to send her away without another word. He'd been thinking of expanding his offices to Seattle. Maybe now would be a good time to move farther afield. He would think about that just as soon as she was gone.

But as she turned and made her way to the door, her face turned from him, a sudden need hit him.

Ellie, he wanted to say, hoping she'd turn and give him just one small smile before she left.

Instead he bit down hard and kept quiet until the door had clicked shut behind her.

What in hell was he doing back here in Red Rose? And why was he wondering if Ellie still slept in the same bedroom she had occupied years ago?

Chapter Five

"I think we need a meeting place, if we're going to have an open house, don't you, Ellie?" Joyce Hives asked the next morning, as Ellie was topping off her third cup of coffee.

"Yes, if we're going to have lots of men floating around, we want a place where we can corral them," Mercy Granahan agreed.

Alarm began to course through Ellie. She and Parker had discussed the realities of what Red Rose could expect. She'd even discussed the facts with the women gathered here, but there still seemed to be some misconceptions.

"I really don't think we're going to have that many men showing up and stampeding around," she began.

"But if we did, we'd want to be prepared, wouldn't we?" Delia asked.

"Well, yes, I'm sure we would, but..."

"What Ellie means is that we shouldn't get our hopes up, Delia," Lydia said gently. "Red Rose is still Red Rose, and not much has changed to make men want to come pouring in. At least not yet."

"I know that," Delia began sadly.

"We can't expect Parker to pull off a miracle," Ellie insisted, knowing that he already felt stressed just being here.

Delia shook her head. "I have faith in him. He just looks like a man who could command other men, don't you think, Ellie?"

"Well, of course, he's a man who can command other men," Sunny said, ignoring the fact that the question hadn't been aimed at her. "He spends his days telling other men what to do. It doesn't have anything to do with his looks, either, because what he looks like is a man who could command *women* to do whatever he damn well pleases. Always was a handsome son of a gun."

"Oh yes," Evangelina Purcell purred. "He's got such broad shoulders."

"And long legs," another woman chimed in.

Rosellen January um-hmmed. "And he's got such a gorgeous flat butt that you'd just love to—"

The door opened and Parker stepped through.

"Touch," Rosellen squeaked, ending her sentence.

Ellie wondered how far she'd get if she ran down the road carrying her coffeepot. She wondered if Parker could have heard anything of what was being said, or if he hadn't, if he wondered why an entire room of women was staring at him with their mouths hanging open and their faces flushing bright pink. All except Sunny, of course, who was laughing heartily.

"You're just the man we wanted to see," Sunny said.

But Ellie wouldn't have agreed. With the image of

Parker's shoulders, long legs and tight…well with the memory of her hands on Parker, she wanted to be anywhere else but here. In fact, she wanted to be anywhere that he wasn't.

"Ladies," he said with a nod. "Beautiful morning, isn't it? And you're all looking as lovely and fresh and…entertaining as ever." He winked at Sunny, but then he turned toward Ellie.

"Ellie? I need to see you. Got a minute?"

Someone took the coffeepot from her hand. Someone else shoved her toward the door. She searched for words.

"You're interfering mightily with my morning job," she said, looking for an innocent subject that didn't involve Parker's anatomy.

But instead of raising his hackles, he only grinned, making her breath catch in her throat. "Good morning, Ellie," he said as he shepherded her outside. "I take it you didn't sleep well last night?"

"How did you know?"

He chuckled. "Other than the grumpy greeting? Oh, no reason. I just got up at two in the morning and saw that there was still a light burning in one of the upstairs rooms in your house."

"Two in the morning?"

"Yeah, I didn't sleep well, either."

"Because…"

He evaded her glance. "Partly because Red Rose is proving to be a challenge. We need to come up with something that sets it apart from other towns."

She sighed. "The only thing that sets it apart is our lack of men and our utter lack of industry."

"Um, Ellie?"

She glanced up.

"Those aren't exactly selling points."

"I know," she said dejectedly. "Do you think we're hopeless? I'm worried about the women. They're pinning their hopes on you as our savior way too much."

"And you're not?"

She shrugged. "I wish you could effect a change, but I'm nothing if not practical."

He leaned close. "Then let's do this practically."

"I don't understand."

"I've got some work I have to do right now that pertains to my business, but…meet me later. We're going to go over this town inch by inch and decide what it is that we can use to our advantage."

"Do you think that will work?"

He stared directly into her eyes. "We're going to make it work."

And for a moment she was just as starry-eyed as all those other women, thinking that Parker could get anyone to do anything.

"Is that what you wanted me for?" she finally forced herself to ask, trying not to keep staring into those golden eyes.

Parker shook his head. "No, I wanted to know who runs the closest and best cleaning service in town. And I don't mean Sunny. That was strictly a personal favor she wanted to perform. Today she's going to be back at The Big Babe."

"The closest cleaning service? That would be…well, that would be…me."

"You run a cleaning service?"

She shook her head. "Parker, women in Red Rose don't have cleaning services. There's no money for that kind of thing. They do their own, but when there are major messes such as trucks that spill things on the roads, messes that are too big for one person, I'm the one who coordinates things and takes care of all that. Why?''

''Isn't it obvious? I need to get started cleaning up the hotel, but Ellie, I don't think—''

''You're not going to start telling me that you think I'm too innocent to be soiled in that way, are you? Or that you think I can't handle the job? Of course, I'm going to do it. I already had it in my plans to head over there as soon as the breakfast shift ended here today.''

''I wouldn't expect you to do this, though.''

''*I* would.'' She did her best to sound wounded, even though lying wasn't built into her genes.

''Well then, I'll pay you well, of course.''

''You will not. We brought you here to help with Red Rose. This is a part of that, and I'll take care of it.''

''I'll expect to help out, too.''

Ellie rolled her eyes. ''Parker, have you ever cleaned anything in your entire life? Has any Monroe ever cleaned anything?''

''I refuse to answer that question, and I can learn.''

She opened her mouth to say no.

''I insist. If you want to use the hotel for guests, those are my terms.''

So what could she say?

''I'll be at your house at ten to see what you've got in the way of mops and buckets. Then we'll stop at the drugstore for cleaning supplies. Be ready.''

''I'll be ready for you,'' he promised, but his voice sounded low and husky. It didn't sound as if he was talking about cleaning bathrooms, so much as it did kissing her clothes off.

And when he turned and walked away, she couldn't help thinking that Rosellen was right about touching Parker's…well, Rosellen was just right. Darn her.

Well, it had been an enlightening day, Parker thought as he knocked on Ellie's door that night. There had been that moment in the Red Rose Café when Ellie was so clearly embarrassed that the ladies had to have been talking about him in either a romantic or prurient way. But she had gotten past that and had, indeed, shown up at his door, prepared to marshal him through the task of cleaning up the hotel.

Clad in a blue-and-white checked blouse and loose jeans that eased against her curves in provocative ways she was no doubt unaware of, Ellie was a picture of fresh-faced loveliness. Her dark curls were hidden under a navy bandana, and he wished she'd remove it, but he couldn't think of one good excuse why she should do so. At least no excuse that didn't involve him expressing the urge to slide his fingers through that dark silk. Instead, he folded his hands behind his back.

"You have mops?" she asked.

"Ah, a woman who cares about my mops," he teased, as he pointed her toward the cache of supplies he'd unearthed from a closet.

She rolled her eyes. "All right, let's go do some damage to all that dust and dirt," she said, her voice sounding somewhat strained.

And for the next few hours, she had worked like a demon, sweeping, dusting, scrubbing floors, washing walls. And still they had only finished a small portion of the hotel.

"Whoa, slow down," he'd told her as she started to rush on to the next task. "It's time to take a break."

"We don't have much time if we're bringing people in here to sleep in less than three weeks."

And he'd gone against all his own good advice and placed his hands on her arms then. "We'll find time," he said, but secretly he was thinking that he'd just find more workers. Still, he wasn't going to say anything about that. It was clear that she would protest.

Now, after insisting that she let him feed her at the Red Rose Café and that he would not allow her to pour coffee or do any other task she normally did while the tables were filled, they were strolling down the short empty streets of Red Rose.

"This is peaceful," he said, as the soft light of evening tinted everything a dusty pink.

"I've always loved this time of day in the summer. It feels like the night is closing us up in a warm pink blanket." Ellie's voice was as soft as a kiss, and Parker wondered what it would be like to curl up in a soft pink blanket with her.

He cleared his throat. "Yes, well..."

"I know. Men aren't into soft pink blankets."

Oh, she was so wrong. With the right woman, men were into lots of things, all of them ending in heat and trouble.

"We'd better get down to business," she continued. "Where do we start?"

He looked around him. "Let's assess what you already have here in Red Rose."

Ellie looked around, her eyes large and worried.

"I'm not sure what we have. I've lived here so long that it's difficult to be objective."

"Well, you've got attractive storefronts, and the town is clean," he began.

"That sounds so boring," she said on a moan.

Parker chuckled. "Relax, we're just starting, Ellie."

"Okay. What else do we have?" They turned the corner and passed in front of the drugstore.

Rosellen January was just locking up. She was chatting with Delia who had just left the flower shop.

"You have women," he said.

Ellie gave him a deadpan look. "That's the problem, Parker. Too many women."

"Do you really think that's the case?"

She looked at the two women and sighed. "No, I love every single one of them. Of us. We're not the problem."

"That's right, you're all a part of the solution. You're a group of enterprising ladies. Besides, hasn't it occurred to you that having lots of women is a draw when you're trying to attract men?"

She stopped in her tracks and looked up at him. "You're not suggesting that we try to seduce men into coming to town?"

Now there was a thought. A sudden picture of Ellie in something tight and red and slinky and very hot slipped into mind and Parker almost had to squeeze his eyes shut to force the image out.

"We're not all governed just by our hormones," he said, knowing his voice came out somewhat grumpy.

"Well, of course not. I just thought—you sounded—"

He waved his hand to stop her. "I'm not going to lie. Men spend an inordinate amount of time thinking about getting women into bed with them, but that wasn't what I was suggesting you capitalize on. I merely meant that you need to assess your strengths. They're here, Ellie. Look at this place. It's quaint and pretty and homey. Men like home, too. I can't think of too many men who wouldn't fall for what you ladies have done to this place. Look at all the flower boxes and the fresh paint. The scent of coffee and home cooking fills the air. I can hear a woman humming in the distance, maybe singing her child to sleep. Things like that, they're big draws, Ellie. Most men would be seduced just by those things." Except for free-ranging men like himself.

"So why did all the men go?"

He blew out a breath. "They needed work. We have to find them work." He'd done his best to jot down lists as they walked. Types of businesses, niches that were already filled, the type of work that might be done and wasn't being done. Unfortunately the last part was very small. These ladies were very self-sufficient.

"I worry, you know," she said.

"You take on too much responsibility. You always did. When you were a little girl, it always seemed as if you were the little mother leading your pack of little sisters around like baby ducks. You're still doing it, only now you're taking care of the rest of the women of this town."

She frowned. "There's nothing wrong with stepping in to do what's needed."

"No, there's not, unless it's making you tense. And

I can tell that it is.'' He reached out then and settled his big palms on her shoulders, kneading gently.

She jumped at first and tried to pull away.

''Shh, just relax, Ellie. I'm not going to do anything. Just this.'' And he continued to stroke and massage.

A small moan escaped her as she gave way a bit. Her skin warmed beneath his hands.

''You're very good at that,'' she mumbled as her head fell back slightly. ''Probably have a lot of practice.''

He would have liked to say no. ''It comes into play now and then.''

A small laugh escaped her. ''You're so modest, Parker. I remember girls who would have died to have you do this to them.''

He couldn't help remembering Mitzi telling him that Ellie had a ''real bad crush'' on him.

''You?'' he couldn't help asking, and she jumped beneath his hands. She practically tried to crawl away.

''Me? No, don't be silly,'' she almost yelled. ''Not me.''

But Mitzi had said yes. Not that it mattered. If Ellie had felt anything like that, she obviously regretted it and thanked her stars for having been saved from him. He'd do well to remember that.

''Be still, Ellie, I'm not done,'' he told her, settling her as he continued to caress her skin, trying to simply think of this as a service he was doing, trying not to think about how satiny her skin was, or how much he wanted to bend and place his lips on that skin. ''I'm sorry I upset you. You and I were always friends.''

''Yes,'' she said, somewhat breathlessly. ''Did I really remind you of a mother duck?''

"The description's apt. How are your sisters, by the way?"

And she opened her eyes wide and stared up into his. He stopped stroking. He froze. Just looking into those gray eyes stole all his thoughts.

"I'm concerned for them," she said. "And maybe in a selfish way. Four of them, Allie, the twins, Becca and Judy, and Suze have already moved away. They couldn't take the feeling that all of the life was draining away. They wanted opportunities and freedom and more life than they could find here. The other two, Lana and Ronnie, married young to the wrong kind of men. They're divorced and still here, but they're starting to lose some of their spark. I don't want them to just fade away and grow bitter here. I want them to have life, too."

She raised her hands and held them out, almost touching him, but not quite. Parker wanted nothing more than to lean forward and make the connection, to drag her close and promise her anything, but she was so earnest, so troubled and he couldn't make promises to her that were bound to disappoint.

"Do you think it's even possible?" she asked.

He knew what she meant. "I don't think Red Rose is ever going to be a boomtown," he said truthfully, "but we're going to do our best to turn things around a bit. That's all I can offer, Ellie."

And maybe then he wouldn't have to spend the rest of his life looking back on this night, seeing Ellie's mournful eyes. If he saved her town, then she wouldn't haunt him when he was gone.

Parker stared at the list on his computer screen. Doctors, lawyers, entrepreneurs, wealthy dreamers.

What could any of them have in common with a place like Red Rose?

He didn't know, but he tagged the ones that were strictly female, feeling a trace of guilt as he clicked the mouse and they exited the screen. Now the list was a bit smaller, but still no less daunting. These weren't people who would be lured to a town by homemade ice cream and fresh-cut flowers and clean streets.

"Damn, damn, damn," he said, getting up to pace. He'd turned whole corporations around, saved businesses on the brink of total ruin, but he couldn't think of one thing that would save Red Rose from the slow death so many small towns faced when their main source of employment had flown. He wasn't the man to save this town. Hadn't his mother hated this place? Hadn't he left, too, so eager to be away that he had never looked back? Who was he to try to sell the place to strangers when he'd run from it himself, and would like to run now?

"Doesn't matter, buddy. You came here in good faith. You're darn well going to do something useful. Keep thinking. Keep looking. There's a key here somewhere." And there was a woman next door waiting. In the dark of night, Parker admitted that Ellie sparked something in him that was fierce and protective and yet animal-like in nature, too. He wanted to please her…because he wanted her.

He groaned, and went to the bathroom to shove his head under the faucet, dousing himself with cold water. Then he paced some more and hoped that the night would bring him answers and the path to free himself from the raw entanglements that Red Rose represented.

* * *

Ellie gazed out at the full moon that rose behind Parker's big old Victorian house, its light shimmering amongst the stars. How many times had she looked out at such a moon in the past few years and been saddened by the thought that no one was next door?

''Well, not tonight,'' she whispered. Every window glowed, the old Monroe homestead lit up like a party. The frantic strains of ''Night on Bald Mountain'' sifted out through an open window somewhere. The man must be crazy to be playing such frenetic music at this hour, Ellie thought, glancing up at the clock that clearly showed that it was past midnight.

Or maybe he wasn't crazy. Maybe he was making wild love with a woman, taking up where he had last left off in Red Rose. There had been plenty of women trailing him around the streets these past few days. Women who had been alone in all the ways that counted for a very long time. Delia had told Ellie that she'd be sending flowers to his house to brighten it up a bit. Other women had been sending their own gifts. They did this partly out of gratitude, but that probably wasn't the only reason, Ellie admitted. Parker was a very desirable man.

And he was a Monroe man. The thought just slid in where it had no business being. But now that it was here, it wouldn't give up. Monroe men, reputed to be more highly charged than other men, capable of giving any woman great pleasure, men who had insatiable appetites. Mick Monroe's had been legendary, had even touched her own family.

Was Parker seducing one of her friends and neighbors in there, moving in rhythm to the fierce strains of the music?

For a moment, Ellie remembered what it was like to have Parker's hands on her, his lips touching hers. Her breathing came fast, her thoughts went blurry, her body ached. And her heart hurt with the loss of something young and innocent, which, she realized, she still cherished.

"Foolish woman," she said. "You're no better than your sisters or Sunny, wanting a man that badly, being discontent with your lot when you've always known what your lot would be."

"Go to bed," she ordered herself. "Forget what he's doing. That's none of your business, anyway. He owes you nothing, not even the thing you brought him here for."

Which was the absolute truth, she thought as she forced herself to move away from the window.

Or almost away, for as she took the first step, Parker appeared in a window next door. The light shone behind him, obscuring his features, but when he stepped back again and the lamplight from inside hit him, she could see that he looked tired. As she watched, he pushed a hand back through his dark hair.

This was not a man engaged in passion, but in a battle of some kind. She wondered if the battle was of her making, related to the task she'd asked him to take on. She remembered all too well that he hadn't wanted to return to Red Rose.

Instantly, Ellie felt guilty, although she had to admit that she also felt a small bit of elation. Parker had most likely not been making love, even though he looked tired.

When Parker had been young, and troubles had hit hard, he liked to drown them in hot chocolate, she remembered. And without another thought, she rushed to the kitchen.

Ten minutes later, she was at his door, knocking to be heard over the noise.

When he pulled back the door, he was frowning. His hair was damp and disheveled, his eyes were cloudy with fatigue and his shirt hung open, revealing a furred and muscular chest.

This was not the boy she'd once known.

Ellie swallowed hard. She held out her offering, a small pot and two cups.

"I saw your light," she said, and thought her words came out sounding weak and lame. What was she wearing, anyway? A pink, fuzzy chenille robe with a hole where the tie at the waist had partially pulled loose. She wished she could cover the bare skin with her hand, but her hands were full. She wondered if she was just one of a long line of pathetic women who had shown up at Parker's door with offerings of food and solace.

"No," she said, then realized she'd said it out loud.

"No?"

Her eyes flew open and she looked up to see the question in Parker's eyes. He still looked tired, but he was grinning.

She swallowed, blinked and shouldered past him, trying not to breathe in his scent or feel his warmth as her barely covered body passed his.

"I saw that you were pacing. I brought hot chocolate to help," she said simply. "Here it is. I'll just be going now." And she put the pot down.

He swore beneath his breath. "I don't bite, Ellie. At least not little rabbits wearing fluffy pink things." He reached out and fingered the sleeve of her robe.

He stole her very breath, and she froze just the way a rabbit did when he realized that a predator was near.

But Parker was no predator. At least not where she was concerned.

''I know you don't bite,'' she said. ''We were never that way.''

He just stared at her, and it was all she could do to keep her eyes from drifting to the bare expanse of his chest.

''We weren't. The hot chocolate will help,'' he finally said with a quick nod. ''Thank you. I was wrestling with the plans.''

''Any luck?''

''Not much. Some.'' He reached behind him and picked up a clipboard from a table. On a legal pad was a list of names.

She shook her head, confused. The names were some of the most prominent men in the country.

''Are these our men?'' she asked.

His eyes zeroed in on her. ''Not exactly.'' His voice was low, almost a whisper. She realized that he had turned the music off. Now all that remained was the big empty house, the darkness outside and the two of them.

''Then who—''

''Potential investors. This one runs a hardware business, this one specializes in electrical components, this man is head of a sporting goods empire. They wouldn't personally move here, but I'd like to see if they might open up satellite industries. Small places that could survive in a place like Red Rose. Places that could hire women, of course, but might also attract men.''

''Why these men?''

He sighed. ''Because these are businesses that Red Rose doesn't already have. You do understand, though, that Red Rose doesn't have any of the attributes that would lead a savvy businessman to relocate a bigger factory here?''

She tilted her head. ''So why would these men come and build?''

He shook his head. ''They might not. They most likely won't, but they might at least be persuaded to try.''

''Why?''

He flinched. ''As a favor.''

''To you. They owe you something?''

Parker turned away. ''In a way. They're all good friends. And I introduced all of them to their wives.''

His voice was flat. She understood. The women these men had married had once been with Parker. They owed their happy marriages to the fact that Parker wasn't a staying kind of man.

It should have shocked her, maybe even cut her.

Instead she laughed. Without thinking, she put down her gifts and threw her arms around Parker.

''You are a genius,'' she told him.

And in less time than it took for her to register the heat in Parker's eyes, he folded her close and kissed her.

''I am totally out of my mind,'' he said.

And then his lips found hers again.

Chapter Six

Parker was kissing her. Ellie's head was swimming, heat and need were rising within her, she was dizzy, but she wasn't so fuzzy that she didn't realize whose lips were moving over hers.

A shiver of pleasure zipped through her, and she raised her hands to place them on Parker's shoulders. She wanted him closer, wanted more of him. And she wanted to tuck her thumbs beneath the cotton of his shirt and feel his skin. She wanted to feel what he had made other women feel, to be the kind of woman Parker would make love to all night. Tonight she wanted to be someone other than herself.

"Oh no." She said the words softly against his lips as reality rushed in, and her body tensed.

And just like that, he pulled away from her. He smoothed her robe down where it had bunched up. He touched her cheek.

"I shouldn't be near you in the middle of the night. People do all kinds of things at night that they would never do during the daytime. You know I didn't mean to touch you."

"I know." Somehow she found her voice, said the words. She even sounded reasonably calm and dignified, even though her heart was hammering and her head was hurting and her pride was ripped wide. She had done what she had always promised herself she would never do. She had let Parker see the needy part of her, the part that had always wanted to be someone else other than Ellie Donahue. "It's all right," she said, her voice growing stronger.

But he shook his head and cupped her jaw. "No, it's not. You and I don't do this. I'm sorry, Ellie. Really. I'll walk you home."

"No, it's just next door."

"Yes, I know. I'm walking you home. Don't come out at night again."

She stopped talking and merely nodded. With great effort she kept her shoulders back and her head high as she turned to march home, the little girl being scolded for being out after curfew.

The evening was beautiful, but she was too aware of Parker moving behind her to appreciate the soft breeze or the starry sky. When they reached her door, she opened it and turned to face him.

"I'm twenty-nine, Parker. This wasn't necessary."

"Then why did you let me come?"

She opened her eyes wide. "Because you felt guilty and this made you feel better. But, Parker?"

"Yes?"

"There was nothing to feel guilty about. I kiss whom I choose to kiss."

"I believe I was the one who chose to do the kissing."

"Yes, but I let you."

"And if you hadn't wanted to let me touch you?"

She lifted one shoulder. "You remember Billy Thornbridge?"

"The kid who kept a running tally of all the girls who dated him and passed out copies to the other boys?"

She looked taken aback. "I didn't know that, but yes, that sounds about like him."

"You're going to tell me that he tried to add you to the list, aren't you? And then I'm going to have to go find him and bust his nose."

"Too late. I already did. So you see, Parker, I could have stopped you from kissing me."

The lamplight shone on his gorgeous face as he lightly touched his nose. "My nose and I thank you then, and—"

"What?"

"Are you saying that you wanted me to kiss you?"

She thought about that. She had always wanted him to kiss her, but only in her dreams, only in the dreams where they were different people and they lived in a fairy-tale world of happy endings. And she had enjoyed his kiss so much, but knew as she'd always known that kissing him would only make her want things she could never have.

"I just wanted to know if all the rumors were true," she finally said, her voice careful.

"What rumors?"

"The ones that said that you were the county's best kisser."

Parker blinked. "Interesting. Well…am I?"

As far as she knew he was the *world's* best kisser.

"I haven't made up my mind yet," she lied, "but, Parker?"

He looked at her, waiting.

"Don't do it again. Please," she said, and this time her voice echoed all the pain and desperation and fear that roiled up within her.

"I won't ever do anything you don't want me to do Ellie," he promised, and he waited for her to go inside and then clicked the door closed behind her.

Inside, she slid down the door and sat on the bare cold floor. She slipped her hands up to cover her eyes and then gradually slid a fingertip down to touch her swollen lips.

"He won't do anything I don't want him to do? That's...good."

Except she had lied. She wanted him to kiss her. Again. And this time she knew how it felt to be held in Parker's arms. So now, the need that had obsessed her for years had grown to mammoth proportions.

She wanted Parker to kiss her, and this time she didn't want him to stop at her lips.

Maybe she should just borrow that list of potential investors from Parker and tell him that he'd done enough. Then he could leave, and she could get back to being a contented virgin again.

The four men Parker had hired arrived the next day in a truck filled with state of the art cleaning equipment. They were followed by a van that brought a decorator and a multitude of wallpaper, carpet and paint samples. The man that stepped from the van was six foot four and looked like he should be wearing six-guns on his hips.

Chester Atchison was the best in the business. He

was also outrageously expensive, but it was worth every penny just to see the expression on Ellie's face when Chester emerged from his princess pink van, a ten gallon feathered hat on his head and a get-out-of-my-way-pilgrim expression on his face.

"Oh yeah," Chester said, looking at the hotel. "This is great. I can damn well do something exciting with this."

Ellie's eyes widened. When Chester marched forward into the building she leaned close to Parker. "What do you think he's going to do with it?"

Parker smiled. "I don't know, but I told him about your museum look idea, and he loved it. Just leave everything to Chester. And those other guys," he said, motioning toward the truck and four-man crew. "Zeb and his men will have the place cleaned up in no time. They're good."

She looked down her nose and crossed her arms, tapping one delicate little foot. "I would have cleaned the place for free."

He grinned and shook his head. "No, you wouldn't have. You think I would have let you slave away and not even paid you? I thought I made myself clear earlier."

She opened her mouth to protest, but he held up one hand. "Doesn't matter anyway. I don't want you on your hands and knees." Big lie. The thought of Ellie on her hands and knees was incredibly erotic and tempting and head-banging, mind-numbing, totally, completely, drive-a-man-crazy-with-need tempting, which was why he wasn't going to allow his thoughts to roam there. "I have other plans for you," he said, and he wasn't sure if he was talking to her or to himself.

"Plans?" Her voice was a croak, and he realized that he must have been looking at her as if he wanted to devour her, which he did, but she was not to know that, ever.

He shook his head to clear his mind. "Not those kinds of plans, El. Come on. I'll show you." And he took her hand and led her to his car.

To her credit, she didn't even flinch or protest. She just followed him, trusted him. Couldn't she see she couldn't trust him? Even he could see that, even though he was offering a million promises to himself never to touch her in any way that moved beyond the bounds of business or simple friendship. And a man didn't offer those kinds of desperate promises if he wasn't *wanting* to do something bad in a very bad way.

Still, she followed him, and her trust made it easier for him to behave himself. He helped her into his car and drove down the road, not stopping until they reached the old factory.

Ellie looked at him, a question in her eyes.

"I'm going to bring Chester over here in a little bit," he told her. "This place is a disgrace. I should have bulldozed it years ago, but now I'm glad I didn't."

"Are you going to reopen it?" Her voice was laced with tentative excitement, and his heart hurt when he turned her way.

"Ellie, I don't know a thing about the shoe industry, and I don't think that kind of factory could survive here. Not anymore."

She swallowed visibly, hard, and he felt like punching himself. "I guess I knew that," she said. "Even if Sunny and Rosellen swear to me that the women of Red Rose spend more money on shoes than any town for miles around. It never really did do all that well, did it?''

He shook his head. ''Marginal, at best.''

''So...?'' She nodded toward the two-story building.

''I thought I'd let Chester clean it up, fix it up and then turn it over to the town as a community center. I know the town doesn't really need one. You do all your meeting at the Red Rose, and that's a lot cozier than this, but at least it will look a hell of a lot better than it does.''

''Parker, you're dropping money into a hole, for nothing.''

He frowned. ''The only other option is to tear it down. It's too out of date for another investor. And if I tear it down, I'm afraid it will distress the ladies. More destruction rather than construction.''

''You're right, but—'' Ellie held out her hands. ''Parker, we didn't mean to get you this involved when we dragged you into this. You'll never see a return on the money you're putting into this place and the hotel.''

''You say that as if I'm not the one at fault for leaving two colossal abandoned buildings in your town for years. I left you to deal with the Monroes' messes. Consider this my very small and inadequate way of making amends.''

''I don't know, I just—''

He broke his new prime rule about keeping his hands to himself and lightly touched his fingertip to Ellie's lips. ''Just think of some good history to feed Chester. I want him to make this fit the town, and you know I never paid any attention to that stuff. Not like you did.''

At last she smiled. ''You were too busy planning what you would do when you left Red Rose.'' He had been. He'd sat in his backyard in the tree house with her and planned out his whole future. She had listened patiently. What an ass he'd been, and no doubt still was.

''Make it right for you, Ellie. Make it right for Red Rose and everyone who lives here.''

She gazed up at him, studying him, her eyes big and solemn and lovely. ''Free rein?'' she finally asked softly.

He nodded. ''Absolutely.''

''All right then. Take me to Chester.''

For a moment, he felt a stubborn urge to say no. Chester's favorite color might be any shade of pink, but he was a man with voracious appetites where women were concerned. Parker didn't want Ellie ending up on Chester's dessert menu.

So when he drove her back, he asked her to give him a minute with the decorator. Pulling Chester aside while Ellie sat in the car, Parker motioned toward her.

''Ellie there is going to provide you with all the background information you should need about the town and about the factory, but that's all she's going to provide you with, understand?''

Chester grinned a big handsome grin. ''You sweet on her, Parker?''

Parker's heart started chugging. He looked at Ellie, her head bent to a pad of paper she had pulled from her purse. ''It's not that way.''

''No? Then what way is it?'' Chester's voice was

laced with disbelief, and he was looking at Ellie with interest that hadn't been there before.

Hell. Parker leaned closer. "It's this way, Chester. I'm her protector. You touch her, you pay, and I take all my pretty money back as well as the chance for you to earn the right to the plum jobs I'm handing you. You touch her, I hire James Loyd."

Chester's brows drew together into a frown. He growled. "Loyd is an idiot. He won't do a good job for you."

"He will if you come on to Ellie."

"I'm the best."

"Agreed. I'd rather have you do this, I'd even considered upping your fee, but…" Parker stared directly into Chester's face.

And suddenly Chester grinned and winked. "Done, for ten percent more than we agreed on. Man, you got it bad, Parker. Truth to tell, she's cute as a miniature rose, but not meaty enough for me. Little too young, too. And anyone can see that she's a lady, not the kind a man makes lewd suggestions to. I didn't have any intention of making a move on her, but now that you've offered me more money if I don't, well…I can see that there's more to her than meets the eye. She does look rather sweet and tasty…."

Parker growled.

Chester chuckled and held up his hands. "I'll be a monk. She'll be just as maidenly when we're done here as when she started, and if she's not, it'll be on your conscience, not mine, buddy."

Parker let out his breath. Slowly, so that Chester couldn't see or hear. "Do a good job on the buildings, Chester."

"That will be a pleasure, my friend. Now bring the little one to me. She and I need to talk."

That sounded ominous, but when he gave Chester a speculative glance, the man only grinned wider. "About history," he clarified. "Lots of dull, boring history that will help me make these sad little buildings come alive. And if the lady loves those buildings, your overseeing their renovation will make her very happy. She'll be exceedingly grateful to you. Who knows what a woman in that situation will do and feel and how she'll express her gratitude to you?"

And with that, followed by a deep, echoing laugh, Chester sauntered over to Parker's car and bent to the window, holding out his hand to Ellie.

Parker didn't know what he said, but Ellie laughed, too. She looked completely free and comfortable when she did, in a way she never looked with him.

He shouldn't care. So, why did he? Parker thought as he left the two of them to begin their project. Maybe he just couldn't stand not having every woman in the world falling over him. His father had been like that. At least his mother had said so often enough. She'd said that he was a lot like his father, too. It was one of the last things she'd said to him before he'd left home.

He'd wanted to ask her to take the words back, but he never had. They barely spoke anymore.

So why did he suddenly find himself pulling out his telephone and calling her at home?

"Parker?" Janette Arlington's voice came over the line, pure and clear and very confused. No wonder. Parker never called her, except on Christmas and her birthday, and maybe, big maybe, on Easter.

''Hello, Mother. Yes, it's me.''

''Well,'' her voice broke a little, ''it's good to hear from you, except…Parker, is something wrong?''

Yes, everything was wrong. He was back in Red Rose and he was having seriously carnal thoughts about Ellie Donahue, a lady he didn't want to harm.

''Everything's fine, Mother. I thought…I just thought you might want to know that I'm in Red Rose. I'm staying at the house.''

''You're in Red Rose? Whatever for?'' Her voice was rising slightly. ''I thought you said you'd never go back.''

He thought about that for a minute. ''I did, I meant it and I'm damned if I know how I ended up here, Mother. Something to do with the ladies of the town wanting someone to bring men back to Red Rose. They want to keep the place alive. They were…convincing.''

To his surprise, his mother chuckled. She never chuckled.

''Mother?''

''I'm sorry, Parker, but you just sound so confused and uncertain. I can't remember a time in your life when you were uncertain about anything. You knew what you wanted and what you didn't want. You were very clear about your preferences in life, and you hated Red Rose from an early age.''

He remembered. He remembered the day that Giles Monroe, his cousin from out of town had come to visit. Giles had been ten years old, just like him, but after only a few hours of playing with the friends Parker had known all his life, Giles had informed Parker that Mick Monroe was a cheating no-good bum and everyone knew it and talked about it. Parker hadn't known. No one had told him. But he'd asked his mother, and she had stammered over an answer that had clearly been a lie meant to make him feel better. She'd sounded so sad. From that day on, he'd hated his father and he'd hated the town. Especially since his father always called him "the chip off the old block."

"Son?"

"I'm here, Mother, and yes, you're right about me and Red Rose, but...here I am. It's only temporary. I'll be gone in a couple of weeks."

"Of course."

"You don't mind that I'm at the house?"

"It's your house, Parker. Your father willed it to you."

"It should have been yours."

"I hated it, anyway. You know that."

Yes, he knew, and he knew why. "I'm...I'm sorry, Mother. Life here was hard for you. Have you...been well?"

"Oh, Parker."

"I know. I never call. Why should I be calling now?"

"I know why you don't call. We won't talk about that, but I'm hoping you've called today because you needed your mother."

Amazingly enough she was right.

"I did."

"Good. Is it very difficult being back there?"

He looked inside himself and was surprised to discover that the answer was no. "It's not that so much. Actually, it feels more like home than I would have thought it would, but Mother, these ladies are counting on me. They need to know that the town isn't

going to fall down around their ears, they think I can work some kind of miracle. I—''

''I know, dear. It was that way for your father, too. He kept that old shoe factory going long after it had headed south. The responsibility pressed on him. That town can be such a burden, can't it?''

His first thought was that, yes, it could be, but no, he didn't think of the women of Red Rose as a burden, especially not Ellie. ''These ladies are just very fragile,'' he explained. ''I'm worried about hurting them, disappointing them.''

''I don't think you will, dear. You're stronger than you think. After all, you were the one who had the guts to leave Red Rose. Your father and I stayed, and look what it did to us.''

''It wasn't the town who hurt you, Mother. It was him.''

For a moment, he thought she hadn't heard him, she was so silent. Then she sighed into the phone. ''Nothing is ever as simple as it seems, Parker. And there are things I wish I could make simple, things I wish I could go back and change, but I can't.''

''You don't need to change anything, Mother. Just be happy.''

''I am happy, son. Very much so. Edward is a good husband and a friend. You...be happy, too. And if I think of any suggestions, I'll call you. That is why you called, isn't it?''

That was what he'd thought, what he'd told himself when he picked up the receiver, but now he knew that wasn't entirely true. ''Partly. Mostly, I think I just wanted to hear your voice. I know that sounds strange.''

''Not to me, son. It sounds wonderful. You take

care now, and don't get too mired down in the problems of Red Rose. It's not your town, anymore. You don't have to do all this.''

But as he said goodbye and hung up the phone, he knew she was wrong. He very definitely had to do all this, because every time he looked at Ellie, she stared back with eyes that were full of faith in him.

What was she going to do when he failed hers?

Chapter Seven

Three days had passed, and Parker was still pacing the floors at night. Ellie saw him through her windows. She longed to go over and ask him how things were progressing, to offer comfort and companionship and hot chocolate, but that would just be courting temptation and disaster, something she'd promised herself and him she wouldn't do anymore. Besides, if something big was on the agenda, Parker would have told her, she hoped. She hated the thought that he might not want to confide in her. For some reason, it hurt, even though it shouldn't have. The man was nothing to her other than an old friend and neighbor.

Still, she could see that he was pushing himself too hard. He was at the hotel and the factory every day, he was on the phone or the computer the rest of the time. Whenever she saw him, he looked like he was on a tether, staying far away, his eyes dark, closing off if she moved too near. The tension within him was a visible thing, and she had done that to him. She was the one who had pulled him away from his good life and brought him here.

And it was wrong for Parker to be shouldering all the responsibility for a town he didn't even like. It was past time for her and the rest of the town to do more.

That was why she found herself standing in the Red Rose Café the next morning, clanging on a metal pot with a serving spoon to get everyone's attention.

''What in the world are you doing, Ellie?'' Sunny asked.

Ellie stopped clanging. ''I'm trying to get all of you to listen to me. We need to talk.''

''About?''

''Men.''

Every woman in the room shut up and sat down. Ellie would have smiled if that hadn't been so sad. ''Actually, it's about Parker,'' she said.

''Does he have good news?'' Delia asked, leaning forward excitedly. ''Has he had answers to those invitations he sent out?''

She hadn't a clue. Parker had been avoiding her for the past couple of days. That probably didn't mean good news.

''The point is,'' she said, avoiding the question, ''when we do have the open house we have to be more ready than we are right now.''

''I'm ready,'' Lydia said. ''Boy, am I ready.''

''You got that right,'' Sunny added. ''The only new man in this town so far is Parker, who doesn't seem to be interested in most of us.'' She emphasized ''most of us,'' looking straight at Ellie, who turned away. ''Oh, and those cleaners and decorators, who just seem eager to get back home. I'm not even mentioning that Chester Atchison. He just rubs me the wrong way.''

Hmmm. Ellie wondered what that meant. She had never known Sunny to let any man rub her the wrong way. ''I don't get it,'' she said.

''He ignored her when she sent out feelers,'' Lydia said. ''No man ignores Sunny.''

''I don't want to talk about him,'' Sunny said. ''Let's get back to Parker.''

Ellie would have rather continued talking about Chester. Parker was too uncomfortable a topic for her. ''What I'm getting at,'' she said, ''is that now that we have Parker here working on the male contact side of things, what more can we do to make this open house a success? Parker's been racking his brain to think of selling points to bring men in, but it seems to me that it's unfair to leave all that up to him. We're the ones who live here, and we're the ones who should be saddled with the responsibility of figuring out how to sell Red Rose. So, what is it that we have that will make men want to come here and stay?''

There was a moment of silence in the room, then Delia turned a bright shade of pink.

''Well, we have...bodies,'' she offered. ''You know, bodies that are different than theirs.''

She sounded so earnest and yet so uncomfortable that Ellie just couldn't smile, though she wanted to. ''Yes,'' she agreed, ''but we're going to assume that they've all seen women's bodies. Even naked ones. Or at least that most of them have. What is it that will make us unique?''

''Damn fine cooking,'' Sunny said. ''Lydia here makes the best regular fare, and I make a mean banana split.''

A chorus of yeses and definitelys followed.

''That's true,'' Ellie said, ''and it makes a great addition, but a lot of these men are from the city where they can get any kind of food they want.''

''Well, what do we need to do, then?'' Joyce Hives asked.

Ellie studied the question. ''I think...we need to do more of what we're already doing. We need to enhance our feminine characteristics, while also making things more appealing to the masculine side of things as well. A woman coming to this town, well, she'd feel right at home. We've got color, flowers, good food, good shopping, a homey atmosphere. Men like some of those things, too, but—I don't know, they must want more. If a man is going to come and build a factory here, then he has to think that there's something here that speaks to the things that make him uniquely male. What is it that men like?''

''We've already named women and food. How about places to hang out with other guys and talk about whatever guys talk about? A place to play poker and stretch out those big hulking frames and scratch themselves if they want to.'' Lydia banged on the table as she finished her speech.

''Ewww, that's such a stereotype,'' Evangelina Purcell said.

''Yeah, I want me one of those stereotypes,'' Sunny said. ''One with muscles, who's big enough not to be intimidated by a large-sized woman.'' She settled her hefty but well-proportioned body deeper into the chair.

Mercy Granahan, who ran the Red Rose Boutique, was frowning. ''Guy stuff, huh? Well...how about sports? We don't have a single sports team here in

Red Rose, and I for one wouldn't mind having one myself, even if the men don't come."

"We don't have enough men to make up a sports team," Rosellen pointed out. "Or at least not enough who can agree on one sport."

"So, we'll make a women's team."

"Will men come and see women play?"

Mercy grinned. "We'll see, won't we? And if they don't come, well, at least we'll have had a little fun ourselves."

Ellie stared down into the reflective surface of the pot she was still holding. "Mercy, I think you have a point. For the past few years, we've just let things slip away. Because we thought our town was dying, we let things go that we shouldn't have. We've got a very fine baseball field that's going unused. We should schedule a baseball game. I'll bet we could get enough players to make up two teams. At least for a friendly game now and then."

"And I could make uniforms," Cynthia Barnette said. "Cute ones with roses on the pockets."

"And we could play music between innings and have a big barbecue and do some of that fun stuff the minor league teams do, like have contests going on before the game."

As the women's enthusiasm caught fire, Ellie felt herself warm inside. If Parker hadn't set her to thinking about what made Red Rose special, she wouldn't have brought up the topic and everyone's eyes wouldn't be lighting up with an interest that was too long gone.

"We should do something with this place, too," Lydia said. "I love it the way it is, but what man would feel comfortable with cream and rose chintz?

We could open up that other dining room I closed off years ago, add some man-size furniture with lots of green and gold and brown, maybe add a wood burning stove for looks in the summer and warmth in the winter. We could set up tables for cards and chess."

"I like chess," Joyce said.

"Great, I don't mean to close off any part of the place to anyone, just make different parts so that people can have a choice," Lydia said.

And as the room began to hum louder, as women jostled to be the first to add some new idea and things began to get frenzied and supercharged and even silly at times, Ellie looked up to see Parker with his hand on the doorknob. For some reason she couldn't possibly understand, her palms turned suddenly sweaty, her chest felt full and her throat tight. She didn't think she could speak to him without embarrassing herself publicly, and so she put down her pan and rushed out the door.

"You sure you want to go in there? They're planning some new ideas. I'm sure they'd like a man to run them past, but…you might want to wait until things calm down a bit."

A smile lit Parker's tired eyes. "I didn't come to see them, anyway. I came for you. You taking that with you?"

He looked down at her hand, and she realized she was still holding the spoon. For a second, she considered putting it back inside, but she was pretty sure that if she went back into the café, she would be caught up in the conversation and never get back out again.

"Guess I am," she said, stuffing it in the pocket of her apron. "Take me as I am, Mr. Monroe."

He didn't say anything for a minute. ''I'll do that.'' And he reached out for her hand. ''Let's go by the hotel. Chester wants your feminine approval on a few things. He said that I had no taste, and you would be better suited for the job.''

She smiled at that. ''Has Chester been decorating the rooms in hues of teal and rose? He told me he was going to do that. He probably figured you'd ask for gray or black or brown. Something very professional.''

He shrugged. ''I might have. I'm a professional and most of the people I deal with think in terms of neutral colors to please the most number of people, but in this case we're not talking a lot of people, and Chester is good at what he does. That's why I brought him here, because he's good at reading the personality of a situation and fitting the decor to suit. So I'm just going to back out and let the two of you decide.''

''That's how you operate? Bring in good people and give them room to run?''

''Usually works. You hire the best, you get the best. And usually, in spite of hiring different people for a variety of jobs, it all comes together in some sort of order to make up a workable plan to ensure a business's success in the end.''

''Order?'' she asked, her voice a bit thin.

''You've got something against order and plans?''

''No.'' She held her hand over her abdomen to calm her nerves which seemed to be threatening to jump out of her body. ''It's just that order doesn't seem to have much to do with Red Rose. Good thing you didn't go into the café back there. We're planning, and order isn't even a small part of it.''

Parker chuckled. ''I can't wait to hear what you've

come up with. After the way all of you overwhelmed me into coming here, I'll bet it's a good plan. What is it?''

And so she told him about the baseball team and the uniforms with roses, the cookout and the changes to the café.

He smiled at first, and then he frowned.

''What?'' Her voice quivered. ''You don't think those things will work, do you?''

He touched her arm. ''It's not that. Not at all. It's a good plan, a sound one. I sense your hand in it all, which means it's a plan that's been thought out more than you're going to acknowledge, but…this business of changing the café…I just—that place means a lot to all of you. It's where you meet, where you go to find solace and friendship and connections. Don't change it too much just to please some men.''

She looked up at him then, and what she saw in his eyes ran deeper than any concerns about the Red Rose Café. She didn't know just what it meant, but she was betting the bank that it had something to do with what had gone on at the Monroe house when Parker was growing up.

''Don't worry. Some things never change, Parker,'' she said softly, and she rose on her toes and kissed him on the cheek. Then she pulled free before she could breathe too deeply of his scent, give in to her need to wrap her arms around him more tightly and offer her lips to him. She began to back away.

He tilted his head, his eyes dark and confused. ''Not coming?''

She shook her head. ''I just thought of something I have to do at the Red Rose.'' A lie. She was running from herself. ''And as for Chester, tell him that I trust your judgement. We brought you here because you'd helped lots of businesses become successes. We trust you, Parker, like you trust Chester. And as for the café, well…maybe the change is a little for us, too. We need shaking up. A little.''

Just not too much, she thought, as she hurried away.

And Parker was more than capable of shaking her world to its very core.

The ladies had worked a miracle in practically no time, Parker thought four days later as he walked into the Red Rose Café. The entry room was much as it had been before, rose and cream colored chintz, lots of plants, warm wood, pink depression glass, tapestry wall hangings and hardwood floors. The room was feminine and charming, but now it opened into a larger room of smoky olive and cream. Roomy chairs were gathered around big tables, and copper etchings accentuated warm tan walls. One half of the room contained small well-lit groupings of tables with chessboards painted in the center. Several papa bear-size rockers, complete with mammoth footstools and cushioned in olive, cozied up to a shiny Franklin stove. A golden sideboard held stacks of books and magazines as well as decks of cards that nested in handmade baskets. It was a room that made a person want to come in and sit down and stay.

''You are all miracle workers,'' he said slowly. ''This place looked fantastic before, but now…damn, if it doesn't look even more inviting. This is the kind of place a person wants to draw near on a cold day. Or a warm one, for that matter. It's big but incredibly inviting. How did you manage to get this done so quickly?

Sunny snorted. "As if you don't know. When you've got Ellie organizing things, well…damn if things don't get done and fast, too. She cracked the whip, and we jumped. Looks great. As good as anything that Chester could have come up with, I'll bet."

Chester, who happened to be standing in the doorway behind Parker, coughed. "It's missing something, girl," he said.

Sunny looked him in the eye. "Are you calling me girl?"

"Are you the one who was talking?"

She ignored the question. "I'll have you know that I'm fifty-three."

Chester raised one eyebrow. He looked her up and down appraisingly. For a second, Parker thought he saw Sunny squirm, but then, he must have been mistaken. Sunny never squirmed. "What's the room missing?" Sunny finally asked.

Chester smiled, the smile of a man used to getting his way with women. "All of the rocking chairs are clearly made for men with lots of room to spread out, a woman's idea of what every man wants. But what if a man wanted his lady close beside him? What then?"

Sunny raised her chin. "Well, maybe he'd just invite her to sit on his lap. Unless he was a man who couldn't take a woman's weight." She kept her chin high, but no one could fail to notice that there weren't many men who wouldn't be cowed by holding someone Sunny's size.

"Well, then, he wouldn't be much of a man, would he?" Chester said with a smile. "Cozying up on a man's lap? That's your solution? I guess I'll have to think about that. It does bear thinking about.''

''Yeah, well that's all you can do with that idea. Just think.''

Chester grinned. And with one last look at Sunny, he left the room.

''Showed him, didn't I?'' Sunny asked, but her eyes strayed to the door. ''A lot of nerve he had, criticizing our idea. I'll bet he thought that I came up with all this, and that was why he was so critical. Ellie deserves all the credit. She's the one who had the best ideas.''

But Ellie was looking uncertain. ''Maybe Chester was right. We designed this room for men, but I don't know the first thing about what men want.''

''Chester is an ass,'' Parker announced. ''He was just trying to get Sunny all riled up. Come with me. You guys carry on. I'm going to steal Ellie,'' Parker told Delia.

''You're always stealing her lately, it seems,'' Lydia said lazily.

That startled him. ''I guess I am,'' he admitted, refusing to think beyond the obvious. ''But maybe that's because you hired her to take me on, so now she's stuck with listening to me.''

Ellie opened her mouth, to protest, he was sure, and he just couldn't help thinking that he'd like to bend over and cover that mouth, to kiss her until she lost all thought of talking, all thought of anything but kissing him back. Still, that was the one thing he wasn't supposed to do, so he just shook his head. ''Come on, Ellie. I have something important to show you.''

''Important?''

"Real important." He pulled her from the room. In the background he could hear Sunny insisting that Chester was not messing her up. No man had ever messed her up, and she was just going to go find him and tell him a thing or two. The door clicked shut on Sunny's next words, muffling the sound.

Ellie ran a step to keep up with Parker, then dropped her apron on a chair on the café's porch just before she stepped down onto the sidewalk. "We seem to spend a lot of time making these sudden exits," she mumbled.

"You don't want to see what I have to show you?"

"See what?"

"I'm not telling. It's a surprise."

She frowned and looked down at their joined hands as if considering whether she should pull away. "A good surprise?"

He laughed and tugged on her arm, leading her to his car. Ten minutes later they were at his house.

She sat up ramrod straight. "I thought we were going to the hotel or the factory."

"What I want you to see is here."

"In your house?" Her voice was high and squeaky. Parker immediately turned to her.

"Relax, El. Just because I've been without a woman for...well, for a while doesn't mean I'm going to start assaulting my neighbors. We're not headed for the house."

"I don't understand."

But he was already circling the car, opening her door, taking her hand and leading her to the backyard. "You might want to take your shoes off if the soles are slippery. Can you still do this, do you think?"

And he motioned toward the tree and the steps that had been hammered into the trunk.

"The tree house? We're going into the tree house? Parker, it must be filled with birds' nests and squirrels' nests and—"

He shook his head. "No, it was built like a fort and it's been closed up tight all these years. There might be some lingering dust, but I was up here not long ago, and I did a rudimentary cleaning job. Come on." And he led her to the steps.

As if she were still ten years old, she kicked off her shoes and climbed. On the first step, her head was as high as his. On the second step, her delicate shoulder blades met his gaze, on the fourth her softly rounded hips, and on the fifth…on the fifth, his breath snagged in his throat as the sweet rounded curves of her bottom came into view. Parker swallowed hard as she moved up, revealing pretty legs and ankles, and then she was above him and he was climbing after her, pursuing her, tumbling into the amazingly spacious area of the tree house his father had paid a carpenter to build for him when he was thirteen and entering the moody, broody I-need-my-own-world teen years.

"Parker, it's…it's…oh, my." Ellie sank to her knees. "It's as if nothing has changed."

"I know. Isn't it great? Things are a bit tattered, but not much different from when we first came up here and set the whole thing up. Remember how I wanted it to be a clubhouse and you insisted on helping me?"

She gave him a stricken look. "I was pretty bossy and bratty, wasn't I?"

"You were cute." His voice softened on the words. "Adorable."

She gazed at him warily. "I was not. You told me that I was taking over when it was your clubhouse. I was pushy."

"You were enthusiastic. I was just...well, a typical teenage boy."

She laughed at that. "You were never a typical anything, Parker. I was a brat. I was like a steamroller, putting up things, adding things. You did *not* like it," she insisted.

He shrugged. "I guess you did scare me a little at the time. You were so intense, so overwhelming for someone so young and so small. You seemed so fragile and you wanted so much."

Ellie looked away. She traced a spot on the wall where a poster had once hung. "I'm sorry I ruined your clubhouse. The other guys wouldn't come around for weeks because I was always here." She sat down in a heap of skirts, looking small and chagrined and contrite and sweet.

What was a guy supposed to do? Parker crawled forward, he sat back on his heels and tucked a finger beneath her chin. He touched his lips to hers. Gently, so very gently, barely letting himself feel the pressure and the desire for her as it started to build within him.

"You made a difference to this place, and the guys who stayed away didn't matter if they couldn't see that."

"You didn't see it."

"I do now. I think I must have even then. Look around, Ellie. Who brought up all these cool pillows? Who told me that I needed a wooden box to keep all my treasures in?" He pulled a box off some shelves built into the wall. ''Who laid down the rugs and hung all the posters on the walls? It wasn't me.''

''The rugs are hideously bright. You had better taste than that.''

''No, I didn't. I didn't know what I wanted. All I knew was that I wanted some space, but what I wanted was a home. You made this a home for me. Look, El.'' He motioned her to a dark corner. From his pocket, he pulled out a flashlight. He touched the small of her back, her skin warm beneath his touch, and she surged forward to the area he indicated.

There on a small table was a candle-fed warming plate, a lantern, a dusty box of games. There in a box was a blanket should he want to sleep out here. There was a small telescope for watching the stars. All Ellie's ideas.

She raised her eyes to his, and in the dusky shadows, she was all pale cream and big eyes and womanly scent. Parker almost had to squeeze his eyes shut to keep from grabbing her and making use of that blanket. Her breathing was coming hard and fast. She was visibly nervous and her eyes skittered away from his, looking at a spot behind him.

She suddenly frowned. ''You kept that?''

Parker looked back over his shoulder where a faded poster of Michael Bolton hung. He grinned. ''The guys gave me tons of grief over that one.''

''Oh, this is embarrassing. Here we have a male, extra-testosterone-required, guys' treehouse, and he was a young girl's daydream.''

''Actually, I thought it was funny at the time, you were so enamored of this guy.''

''Parker…''

He reached, pulled her close. ''Don't be embarrassed, Ellie. You were such an endearing child.''

And she froze in his arms. He knew why. She didn't want him touching her. He'd promised he wouldn't. Immediately he let her go, even though his hands felt empty, his body bereft.

Ellie sat back on her heels. She shook her head. ''Well, I know I was a pest even though you're being nice about it. The truth is that I lied to you earlier. When I was young I *did* have a bit of a silly crush on you.''

''I know.''

She took a deep and noisy breath. Those gray eyes turned panicky. She looked like she wanted to run, maybe to jump out the window. ''You know? You knew then?''

''It's okay, Ellie. I didn't know until you were older and past all that. You must have already been sixteen or seventeen by the time I found out. You must have confided in Mitzi, and she let it slip. I was pretty ticked off at her for telling your secrets and I'm afraid to say that I yelled at her.''

''You must have been so disgusted.''

''Well, she shouldn't have been repeating something I'm sure you hadn't wanted anyone to know.''

''I don't mean about that, Parker. You must have been disgusted to think that I was acting like your friend while I was nursing a crush.''

''You *were* my friend, Ellie, and I was, I don't know, honored that you had chosen me to have a crush on. Scared, too, a little. Even back then, when we were in our teens, I'd known that you were off limits. I respected you too much to ever think of you that way. We both knew that I wasn't like other guys and never would be. I never wanted to be.''

''And still don't,'' she said quietly.

''And still don't,'' he agreed.

She raised her hand and touched his cheek. She leaned forward and kissed his other cheek and he breathed deeply of her scent. For a moment he felt as if he could stay that way forever. Just breathing the air she breathed.

But then she pulled back. ''We should take this down.'' And she reached for the poster.

''No, don't. Leave it. It's a moment in history. Our history. I brought you here to show you that you'd made a difference in my world when I was young, Ellie. And to tell you…that job you did today at the Red Rose? It was phenomenal. You are phenomenal. Don't let someone like Chester tell you different. He's just sexually frustrated because he wants to sleep with Sunny and he doesn't think she's the kind to play around, so he's taking his anger out on everyone.''

She blinked.

''Men do that, Ellie. You know it.''

''I know, but still, I was totally flying blind on that café thing, Parker. I didn't even ask for your input.''

''You didn't need it, El. You have good instincts. Look at this place. You did a good job. You were younger than me, but you had fire and dreams. You introduced me to things I wouldn't have tried. You gave this place personality, you brought some brightness into my life. I hope some day you find a man who will appreciate you.''

She shook her head so hard that her dark curls danced around her. ''You know I don't want a husband.''

"Who said you had to have a husband? I only said that you should have a man who would see you for all the wonderful things you are and who would show you..."

His voice trailed off, she was looking at him with those big, pretty eyes. "Show me?" she asked on a breath.

And he leaned forward. "Yes, show you how desirable you are," he whispered, and he framed her face with his hands, he covered her mouth with his. He showed her how very much he wanted to touch her.

Her hands climbed to his elbows and then she pushed them up his chest. When he retreated for breath, she clutched his shirt and pulled herself to him, her lips like soft rosebuds that parted beneath his mouth.

She tasted of cinnamon, she tasted like no woman he'd ever tasted before. She *was* like no woman he'd ever tasted before, and he wanted her beyond belief, but they were here where they'd been children and where the memories of her childhood crush made her vulnerable.

He had to have her.

He had to stop.

It would kill him, he would go crazy.

And if he hurt her, he would go crazier still.

With a strength he would have sworn he didn't have, Parker wrenched himself away from her.

"This plan of ours had damn well better work, Ellie. This town had better become every bit what all of you want it to be, because when I go, I'm never coming back. I can't come back ever again, do you understand?"

''Yes.'' Her voice was a sob. He hated himself for doing that to her.

And so he kissed her once more, gently. So gently it was barely a touch.

''You gave me something good here, once, Ellie. I swear I'm going to give you what you want before I leave.''

And he led her from this place they had shared so long ago. He promised himself he would never come up here again.

Chapter Eight

Well, this was it. He had put the call out for friends from all over the country. He had even heard back from a few, Parker mused four days later. Some just couldn't make it, some agreed to come because he was a friend or a business associate who had done good things for them in the past. Not one seemed to express even the slightest inclination to come to rural Illinois and set up a new operation, no matter how small.

He couldn't blame them. There was no real profit to be made here, at least not on a major scale.

"Hell," he said, throwing the list of RSVPs down on his desk. "This isn't good enough, Monroe. Try harder, reach deeper. Look at this the way Ellie would have years ago. There's more to this town than a profit center. What kind of person would respond to what Red Rose has to offer?"

Family men, men who liked comfort, men who wanted wives and good food and things that were homey, men who'd made careers out of starting small and building up.

Well, heck, he'd tried that tack already. Maybe some of these men on the list would stick, and maybe none of them would. There wasn't anyone else left to try.

Except those who didn't like small, or homey, or small-town slow. Men who didn't want wives or commitment.

Ellie and the ladies wouldn't thank him for bringing those kind to town.

But if there was one thing he'd learned over the years, it was to try all angles, go out on a limb, jump off the roof and start a riot if nothing else worked.

Sometimes something happened. And sometimes he had to do damage control.

He didn't want Ellie getting damaged or caught up in a riot, but he couldn't leave here knowing he hadn't done all that he could.

There were still a few people he knew that he could contact. No pretty letters this time. This was going to involve some serious arm-twisting.

Things could get ugly. It was a risk.

He thought of Ellie's face lighting up years ago when she'd steamrollered his tree house, his personal space, when he'd thought she was cute but crazy. He'd known darn well he was risking his reputation with the guys.

He'd let her get away with her plans anyway.

He'd had to put up with plenty of ribbing.

It had been worth it.

"So, let's do something wild and risky," he told himself as he pulled out his address book and prepared to bring the bad boys in.

What in hell was Ellie going to say?

* * *

Things were getting crazy around town, Ellie couldn't help noticing after three more days had gone by. Parker was driving Chester and the work crews like crazy, trying to make sure everything was done on time. When she asked him about who was attending, he slid around the issue, never committing, never telling her much.

But he looked worried. He certainly didn't look like the teasing Parker she'd known. And he definitely didn't kiss her again.

He'd known that was a mistake. He'd told her that he couldn't be touching her. The fact that he had, the fact that she'd touched him, too, and the fact that they both wanted to climb into a bed together didn't matter. As children, they had known their destinies lay down different paths, and none of that had changed.

Parker was trying to be good. She should be grateful, but she was on edge.

Heck, everyone was on edge. The whole town was going nuts with cleaning and sewing and baseball practices and cooking and painting. The town had never shined this much. Sunny had gotten up on a ladder and polished Big Babe, and now the statue's boobs sparkled like mirrors, drawing even more attention to the mammoth woman. They'd be lucky if some prospective investor didn't drive into a ditch when he got his first glimpse.

"Damn, this place looks good. I like those flyers you had printed up, too," Sunny said to Ellie the next morning in the café.

"Well, the girls have been practicing their pitching and hitting and Cynthia Barnette has sewn up those uniforms, Lydia's planning all that food and a big raffle at the new community center. It would be a shame if no one knew how to get to the field. Besides, everyone's worked so hard, I wanted to point out every business and every point of interest in Red Rose. We're going for broke on this one. Once the men come into town, we either sink or we swim on presentation.''

''Does he have a lot of men, do you think?''

Ellie took a deep breath. Parker had told her that he had responses, but that she shouldn't expect a miracle. He'd apparently had many negative responses as well.

''Parker says we'll have a decent-size group.'' Which didn't say much, but she didn't want to pump him for more information. He was starting to have that tense look he sometimes had as a young man. That had usually happened right after Mick Monroe took up with someone new and while Parker's mother was wearing that haunted look. She remembered one time hearing Parker yelling at his father and Mick laughing and telling him that he liked his son's fire. It reminded him of his own when he was a young man. She'd seen Parker leave the house and go to the tree house right afterwards. She hadn't seen him for several days after that, but she'd known something of what he was feeling. She'd always supposed that he felt pretty hopeless to change his parents' situation, because she had felt that way about her parents before her father died.

She rather felt that same way about this situation now. There wasn't much more she could do.

She supposed Parker couldn't, either. He had, after all, told her that the town's position wasn't good. That probably didn't make him feel any better now that the final day was drawing near.

"Ellie?"

"What!" she barked, whirling to meet Delia's innocent stare. Delia's eyes widened and turned watery.

Ellie shook her head. "I'm sorry, Delia. I'm just tense. It's me, not you."

"I'm tense, too," Delia whispered. "We've worked so hard, but it's all so small town. What if all those big city men laugh at us?"

"They laugh and I'll break some arms," Sunny said.

A general grumbling agreement followed. The word "men" was repeated numerous times, and not with sympathy, either. After all, it had been men who had caused all their problems in the first place.

Right then the door opened, and sixty-eight-year-old Albert Stiles strolled in. "Coffee hot?" he asked, looking hopefully toward Lydia.

"Hot enough to burn your hair off if I decided to pour it on your head," Lydia said, staring at Albert like prey down the barrel of a shotgun.

"Can't you see we're busy, Albert?" Joyce Hives said. "We're neglecting our own businesses to finish getting ready for the big do. We don't have time to serve you coffee. Come back later."

These last words were said with a scowl, and when Albert slipped out meekly, Joyce brushed off her hands as if she'd just chased the vermin out. Then she took a deep breath. She blinked several times.

"Oh dear," she said. "That wasn't very nice of me, was it?"

"Yes, well I was the one who threatened to pour

hot coffee on his head, poor old dear,'' Lydia said. ''And Albert's such a meek man, too.''

''Look at us,'' Delia said. ''We're all so edgy, we're picking on the only good men the town has left. We're alienating the people we love and the men who've been faithful. I was ready to go after him with a broom myself. What's wrong with us?''

''Nerves,'' Sunny said. She looked at Ellie for confirmation.

''Major nerves,'' Ellie agreed. ''We've just been going at this so hard that we're strung far too tight. This can't be good.''

''No. All those men are going to come to town and find a bunch of...well, you know, the word that rhymes with witches.''

''Can't have that,'' Lydia said.

''We need to relax,'' Delia agreed.

''Okay, okay, okay, how do we do that?'' Joyce was looking miserable, staring at the point where Albert had disappeared out the door.

''Only one way,'' Sunny said, rising from her seat.

''Definitely only one way,'' Lydia said, turning the Open sign to Closed and picking up her purse.

Joyce cocked her head, confused. She looked at Lydia.

''Shopping,'' Lydia said. ''Lots of shopping. Have to buy things. Clothing. Perfume. And best of all... shoes. Many pairs. Many styles. Man-killer shoes.''

A chorus of oohs and ahs ensued, and smiles began to form. Ellie didn't know if it was the specter of the old shoe factory or what, but Red Rose women sure loved their shoes.

''Come on, girls,'' Lydia continued. ''Just as soon

as we can get ready, we're heading out of town to the nearest mall. We're going to go out and buy, buy, buy until we've forgotten all about our big plans, and then tomorrow we're going to come back and get ourselves ready for the fact that we're about to be invaded by men. This incident with Albert has made me realize that we have to be prepared. Over the past few years we strong-willed women have become even more strong-willed and now we're hoping to import a bunch of strong-willed men. We have to decide how we're going to start out with them, because the way we start is the way we end. We don't want to cowtow, but we don't want to send them running the way we just did with Albert. Lots of stuff to think about, but if I'm going to think, I have to have new clothes to do it in. New high heels."

"New lingerie," Sunny agreed. "Let's go. I'll go find Jarod Rodgers and ask him to lend us the schoolbus. You all coming?"

Ellie smiled. The energy emanating from the group of women grabbing up their purses could power a small town for a year. Shopping sounded lovely, but she shook her head. Quiet sounded better.

"You know I never did get into shopping as much as all of you. I'm going to meditate. Same effect for me," she declared.

Sunny wrinkled her nose. "Meditation has its limits. I'll bring you back something cute and sexy."

And Ellie knew why she wasn't getting into the swing. She alone was not looking to make herself pretty for a man. "Thank you, but there's no need."

Sunny stared her down. "You don't look dead, and if you're a woman and alive, there's a need. You'll wear whatever sexy thing I bring you, and you'll feel better for knowing that you have a lacy red thong on under your blue jeans.'' And with that, she swung her massive frame around and led her chicks out the door.

In fifteen minutes flat, every businesswoman in Red Rose had taken in her shingle, and Ellie was left standing alone outside the café as a trail of dust plumed out behind the bright yellow bus.

''Fire somewhere?''

Ellie jumped and turned to look at Parker.

''Worse. Shopping trip to the mall. Very urgent.''

He gave her a speculative smile. ''Not for you?''

She shook her head. ''I don't shop. At least not for fun.''

''No? What do you do? For fun?'' His voice dipped low.

Ellie took a deep breath. It suddenly occurred to her that the town was a lot emptier without the women around her. There was a lot less insulation between Parker and herself. At the moment, they were practically alone, and Red Rose seemed suddenly dangerous in a way it never had before.

''I...work,'' she said.

''For fun? Really?'' He frowned, disbelieving.

Why should he believe her? She was lying. She just hadn't been able to think of a quick answer that didn't involve her body touching his. Now, however, she was committed to this course of action.

''Sure,'' she said with more certainty, tossing her head. ''I'll bet I can find something fun to do, some little tidbits of work left to do before the strangers come in and time to prepare runs out.''

''Sure. Still things to do.'' He held up a piece of paper he was holding, rattling it.

Oh. He was still working. This was her town, but he was the one still working.

"What are you going to do?" she asked.

"Go check out the hotel and the community center. Make one last pass. Make sure everything's done."

"I can help with that."

"You don't have to."

"I want to," and she realized that she was telling the truth. "Where do we start?"

"The community center first. Chester might still be finishing up at the hotel. I want to go through after his men are done."

So they drove in silence to the old red brick building. It looked different now. Fresh. Alive. Pampered, the brick sandblasted and clean, a new, shiny sign declaring that this was the Red Rose Community Center. Landscapers had planted flowers and bushes and trees outside. They'd made a brick walkway and added benches along the path.

"Who would have thought the old shoe factory would dress up so nice," she said. "You sure you want to turn this over to the town?"

"It belongs to the town. You've all put up with it in bad times. Now take it and use it in better times."

"Will they be better, do you think?" She turned and looked at him.

He gazed directly into her eyes. "I don't know, Ellie. I honestly don't know, but...I hope they will. I hope you'll get what you want from all this work. You'll have to write me and let me know how things are going."

A lump settled right in her throat, making it almost impossible to speak. Soon he would be back in his world and she would he here, carrying on.

"I'll do that," she said. And they traveled the building in silence, touching the new wood trim, gazing up at the pictures of the town's forefathers that had been hung here. Parker hadn't wanted his father's picture there, but the ladies had insisted. Mick Monroe, no matter what he had been, had been a part of Red Rose history. This had been his factory. And, as Sunny pointed out, you couldn't leave holes in your history.

But that was what Ellie felt she was doing as they got back in Parker's car and drove to the hotel. She was going to leave holes in her own history, because Parker was a part of it, and he had always been a part that brought tears to her throat. He was the part that was always on his way out of town, and she didn't think she could bear to think of him too often.

They sat in front of the hotel for a few minutes, just staring. A low, tasteful sign now declared this to be the Red Rose Heaven Hotel. The building looked…reborn.

"Chester certainly knows how to put on a show, doesn't he?" she asked. "He must have brought in an army to complete this."

"He did, and he enjoyed every minute of it."

The building was still pink, but it had been sandblasted and softened by cream and gold trim. He'd added some Greek Revival style elements, added a new entranceway that extended out from the building with a gilded gable and columns entwined with vines. The asphalt parking lot had been torn up and replaced with grass and walkways and fountains containing Greek statuary that spouted water. A newer, less obtrusive parking area edged in greenery had been placed behind the building. The whole affair had an air of age and elegance, but was still amazingly sensual, maybe more so than the original.

Ellie followed Parker inside. The lobby was done up in cream and teal with touches of rose and lots of deep cushy sofas. More fountains as well as display cases containing some of the original Honeymoon Suites From Heaven artwork. What had looked tacky before looked tasteful now.

"He's a wizard," she said simply. "I wonder what he could do with my house."

She turned to smile at Parker, but found he wasn't smiling. "Don't allow yourself to be alone with Chester. He's done a good job with this place, and that's partly because, yes, he is a wizard, but it's also because he's a man who thrives on the pleasures of the flesh. He had a blast turning my father's love nest into something that looks almost classy. Don't close yourself up in a room with him."

Ellie blinked. "I hardly think Chester would jump me. I don't think I'm his type."

Parker groaned. "You're every man's type. You're not a type. You're just Ellie, and that means you're desirable. Come on, let's stop talking about this before I do something crazy."

And he reached out to take her hand, then changed his mind and motioned her to precede him down the hall. He opened the first bedroom, and Ellie peered inside.

"Oh my. Oh, Parker." She stepped into a room that looked like it had been built of cream. The carpeting, the bed coverings, the walls, all were in the same rich color, only the walls reflecting splashes of color. Here was art, real art, depicting mythological creatures in deep rich tones of red and gold and white and flesh tones. Here were the lovers, Eros and Psyche, Perseus and Andromeda.

The paintings were perfectly innocent, very tasteful, but in their own way they were more sensual than anything Mick Monroe had put here. A person could close themselves up in such a room and just stay here for a week or a month, alone or with a partner, and be utterly content.

"This is so lovely," she said, whirling around and finding Parker right behind her. Or rather, in front of her as she practically jumped up and down on her toes. "This is luscious, don't you think?" And she smiled up at him and leaned forward.

Parker groaned. "I'll tell you later. Right now I can't think, Ellie." And he took the hands she was holding out. He placed them on his chest and he wrapped his arms around her. He kissed her, and his kiss was richer even than the room.

Parker's touch ignited every daring wish she'd ever had. His eyes on hers were hotter than eyes had a right to be. Her insides were melting with delicious pleasure.

She rose on her toes and kissed him with all that she had and all that she was, and slowly, slowly, they sank down to sit on the edge of the bed.

"Ellie, tell me to stop kissing you."

"Kiss me more, Parker."

"If you don't stop me, I don't trust myself to do the right thing. I'll take this too far. I'm still the same man I always was. I'm a Monroe. Ruthless and unethical where women are concerned. No control. I don't trust myself, Ellie. I would take you, tangle my body with yours and toss you aside without looking back.

Don't let me do that.'' He pulled back, so that his lips were a full six inches away.

And she cried out. Always, always, she had been wanting Parker, and he had always been moving away. Now he was here, he was telling her he wanted her, even if it was only for this moment. And she had to have him. She couldn't go through life not knowing what it was to be desired by him.

Bravely, she raised her chin. She ventured a smile. ''No one has ever wanted to tangle with me that badly. I wonder what it would be like to have you touch me like that, Parker. I'm older than I used to be, I've missed a lot, and I don't want to miss more. I'm not a risk-taker or an adventurous sort, and there's a lot I haven't experienced. It seems to me that it wouldn't hurt for me to experience some of the things I've missed. Tangle with me, Parker.''

He closed his eyes as she moved closer, her lips hovering near his.

''I don't want you to be hurt.''

''You never did, and that was fine. I was a child then. Now I'm not. Now I choose to risk it.'' And she plunged her hands into his hair, she pulled him to her. They fell back on the bed and his lips found hers, burned hers, branded hers.

Parker skimmed his hands up her sides, beneath her blouse. His hands found her breasts, grazing the sensitive skin, then moving away as she arched and moaned at the thought of losing that amazing touch.

He kissed her again. This time his fingers deftly unfastened her buttons. Her breasts rose and fell beneath the thin white chemise she wore.

''Ellie,'' he said, and he bent to kiss her breast through the cloth. Her nipple puckered as he suckled her. Sensation, desire rippled through her. She wrenched the straps of her chemise down, baring herself to him, and he caught her breasts in his cupped hands.

"El, you're magic," he said on a breath, as his thumbs feathered over her skin. And then his lips were on hers again, he was stroking her, kissing her, driving her mad until she thought she would cry with the wonder of being here with him. He slid one hand up, cupping her thigh. His thumb edged higher. She wanted to scream with the need for him.

A car door slammed outside.

Ellie gasped.

"Hell." The word left Parker's mouth like a small explosion. In five seconds flat he had smoothed her clothes back in place and buttoned her buttons.

He looked down at her and kissed her gently one more time. He took her chin in his hand. She looked up into his eyes and saw pain, regret, anger.

"Ellie, this is for the best. I don't want this with you."

She thought she would die from the pain, but he took her by the shoulders. "Damn it, don't look that way. You know darn well what I mean. I want you, it's so hellishly obvious how overwhelmingly I want you, but…I can't do this, El. It would kill me to treat you the way Mick Monroe treated the women of this town. You understand?"

She bit her lip and nodded meekly, trying to keep the tears from her eyes. She understood. He desired her, but he did not want to give in. He was asking her to help him fight the thing that was between them.

She had always done her best to be true to Parker. "No more tangling, ever," she agreed.

He nodded, and breathed out raggedly. "All right, let's go see who that is. Whoever it is, I owe him one."

Chapter Nine

Who the heck was out there? Parker wondered. Probably Chester, coming back to check on something, and Chester was the last person Parker wanted Ellie to have to encounter right now.

"Just wait here, El. Relax. I'll see who it is," he said.

She gave a quick nod, so leaving her to gather her wits about her, Parker stepped out into the parking lot of the hotel. What he saw made him blink, and if he'd been the kind of man to let his jaw drop in surprise, he would have. There, getting out of a black Mercedes was Griffin O'Dell, an old friend and the last man Parker had ever expected to take him up on his offer to come to Red Rose. Griffin was strictly big city, strictly big business and after a hellishly messy divorce and custody battle, the last thing he wanted was a bride.

"Griff, what are you doing here?" Parker asked, sticking out his hand.

Griffin shook his head tightly. ''Damned if I know. You called. I came.''

But he had called a lot of people, and there were plenty who weren't planning on showing up. Griffin had been a long shot, a desperate move to swing his net out as far and wide as he could, Parker thought. If Griff had come, then anyone might show up.

Then Griff chuckled. ''Don't worry, the world isn't spinning out of control. I was on my way to Chicago for a meeting, anyway. This was only a few hours out of my way. I thought it would be interesting to come see what it was that had you so uncharacteristically discombobulated. And now I see what it is,'' he said, looking past Parker's shoulder.

Parker turned to see Ellie emerging from the hotel, her eyes wary, her fingers still plucking at her skirt as if she was afraid that someone could see that she had just been rolling on a bed with a man. And he supposed someone could if that someone knew what to look for. Her lips definitely looked well kissed.

''Griffin, I'd like you to meet a friend of mine. This is Ellie Donahue. We go way back.'' He didn't elaborate. Griffin was already looking too pleased with himself. ''And Ellie, this is Griffin O'Dell. We met in college and still stay in touch.''

Griffin held out his hand. ''Parker's being polite. I've never been a very good one for staying in touch. I travel too much, but he always manages to talk me into standing still for at least a few hours now and then. I'm glad I got the chance to meet someone who goes way back with Parker.'' He shook the hand that Ellie offered, then turned it over and studied her fingers. Parker knew what was up. Griffin was looking for a ring. Because he thought Parker was interested in Ellie or because he was? His divorce had been final almost a year ago.

Parker felt a growl crawling up his throat. He stifled it.

"Oh, I'm so glad you came," Ellie said with true enthusiasm. She smiled up into Griff's eyes, and it was all Parker could do to keep from stepping between them. "I knew Parker would come through for us. He's worked so hard. Will you be staying long? Do you have a room here at the hotel? I mean, I know Parker's been hiring people and there's a skeleton staff ready to come on board tomorrow, but I'm not sure...we could maybe..."

Parker smiled. "Don't worry, El. I've got it covered. Griff can stay with me."

"Oh no, Parker. That's just not right," Griffin protested. "I dropped out of nowhere. Didn't even call. I'll admit that I stopped at this place on a whim, just because it was there, but if it's not ready, I'll find someplace else."

Which brought a chuckle from Ellie. "Better take Parker up on his offer. There is no place else, although the hotel will be opening up in two days. You are here for the open house?"

"Actually, I'm just here to see Parker, though I'm intrigued enough to stay for the open house. Sounds like an interesting project you've thrown together. Then I'm on my way back to Chicago."

Parker studied Ellie carefully and noted that she didn't let her disappointment show. Well, that was his Ellie. She could always be counted on to be calm. Unless a man was kissing her.

Ouch! Where had that thought come from? Better steer his mind into saner paths, like thinking about the fact that he had been right about Griff. He wasn't here to do business.

"Come on, Ellie. I'll drive you home. Then I'll give Griff the three dollar tour, feed him and take him back to my place."

"I'll send over food," she said. "I know Lydia's been sending over meals for you, but Lydia is otherwise occupied, as you know."

He shook his head. "You don't have to do that, Ellie."

She placed her hands on her hips and leaned toward him, her gray eyes solemn, one brow raised imperiously. She was cute as hell, all five foot four of her. "Parker Nathan Monroe. I lure you here, take up your time and heaven knows how much money with all the renovations you've done. You bring in guests," she said, nodding curtly toward Griffin, "and you think it's too much trouble for me to make you a meal? This is Red Rose, and hospitality and gratitude and loyalty are important to us. I most certainly do have to make your dinner. And you and Mr. O'Dell have to eat it." She crossed her arms and smiled slightly.

Parker exchanged a look with Griffin. "She may be small, but she's mighty, O'Dell. Be prepared to eat a home-cooked meal." Then he smiled at Ellie. "Have I told you how pushy you are lately?"

She grinned. "I'll take that as a compliment."

"I meant it as one."

"Good. Now take me home so I can cook. And make sure you give Griff the good tour, not the B.B. one."

For a moment, Parker shook his head, confused. Then he realized she was talking about the shiny statue in front of Sunny's business. ''I don't know. I think Griff might like seeing the B.B.''

She looked at Griffin's tasteful business attire and frowned skeptically. ''I don't want him to run away before his visit is officially over. How do you feel about twenty-foot-tall women, Mr. O'Dell?''

Griff blinked, then did a hasty recovery. ''Love 'em. Parker, why didn't you tell me the town was populated with Amazons? Now this I've got to see.''

And laughing, the three of them got into Parker's car and drove away. Fifteen minutes after dropping Ellie off, Parker pulled over and turned to Griffin.

''You didn't just stop by, did you?''

Griffin shrugged. ''Alicia is giving me problems about Casey. Even though I have summer visiting privileges, she insisted she had to have him this week. Something about a dreadfully important trip to her mother's. She's doing all she can to find new ways to take him completely away from me. I could take her to court again, but that's so hard on Casey. So I gave in and now I'm kicking myself and missing him like crazy. I just had to get away for a few days. Seeing an old friend seemed like a good bet.''

Parker nodded. ''I'm glad you came. It's been too long. So...what do you think of Red Rose?''

Griffin shrugged. ''It's...pleasant, small, probably full of good kind souls with good intentions.''

''Not your cup of tea, eh?''

Griff looked wary. ''This is your hometown, Parker. I'm not going to dis it. And it does seem nice enough. I hope you get someone to make an investment in the place. If anyone can, you can. Or your pretty little friend can. She's absolutely charming. And achingly lovely. Not attached, I take it?''

Parker leveled a look at Griff. "Not attached. To anyone, including me. That doesn't mean she's fair game."

Griff held up his hands. "I'm not here to play, Parker. I'm here to hide."

"From Alicia?"

"Not really. More like...from myself. But hiding never works for long. I've got to be back home in four days. Casey will be coming back. How long are you going to be here?"

Parker faced the truth. "Not long. Once the open house is over, I'll have done all I can. Red Rose will either fly or it will settle down to shut its doors quietly."

"And how will the little beauty feel about that? About your leaving them?"

Parker shook his head. "Ellie and I need to be apart. We don't do well together for long." Because when they were together, he had a bad habit of wrapping his body around hers and peeling back her clothing.

Griff smiled and shrugged. "Same old Parker. Here today, gone tomorrow. We're two of a kind, buddy."

That they were. Which meant that no matter how much he liked Griff, he was going to keep an eye on him. He hadn't spent his life protecting Ellie from himself only to let some other man harm her.

Hours later, Parker sat on Ellie's porch. Griffin was borrowing Parker's office to do some work.

"He seems like a nice man," Ellie offered.

Parker smiled in the dark. "He really isn't staying, Ellie. Griffin is the last man who would want to stay in a place where he might be constantly considered a candidate for marriage. His divorce was so nasty and the custody battle so ugly and harmful that he'd never willingly go near the institution of marriage again. Red Rose is a great little town, but not for a man like Griffin. Besides, his sporting goods business has expanded so much in the past few years that he told me last year he was not going to build any more for a long time. We're striking out on all counts here.''

''Oh, I don't know. You get to see an old friend. That counts for something, doesn't it?''

He ran one fingertip down her cheek. ''Old friends count for a great deal. I'll want to know how things go, you know, how things have worked out for everyone. You'll send me a message when the smoke has cleared, won't you?''

She trembled beneath his touch. ''I'll call your receptionist and leave a message,'' she agreed. Which wasn't at all what he meant, but then, what did he mean? What good could it do, continuing any kind of contact with her when he knew darn well that once he was back in Chicago, he'd be back to his old ways.

It wasn't fair to hold her to anything. That was too much like his father, wanting his wife to be a constant in his life while continuing to lead his life just as if he weren't married. The no-commitment Monroes. They were considered leaders in life. What kind of leaders were they, though?

''I want to know how things turn out here,'' he said aloud, and he wasn't sure if he was talking to Ellie or himself.

''I promised, I'll let you know,'' she said, her voice a whisper.

And Ellie, unlike the Monroes, always kept her promises. She lived up to her end of a bargain when a bargain had been made. Had he done that here?

He'd come, he'd planned, he'd built, he'd invited, but now he was leaving. No matter the outcome of the open house, he wasn't sticking around.

Wasn't that just like a Monroe? Cut and run when things got sticky.

Damn straight, he thought. Sometimes the only thing you could do was cut and run.

There was something different about today, Ellie thought, when she first woke up three days later and heard the sound of traffic outside her window. Oh yeah, today was the day of the open house. Tomorrow, or maybe the day after, was the day Parker would step out of all of their lives once more.

Her elation at knowing that all of their plans had come to fruition quickly faded.

"Don't do this," she told herself. "You knew he was only here for the short-term. He made you no promises." And never had. She wasn't supposed to want promises from him. She'd told herself that all her life. For the past eleven years she'd done just fine without him here. So why was she acting so glum now?

"Probably just the anticlimactic effect of having a big job come to an end," she figured. Sure that was it. Anytime a person dove headfirst into a big project there was always a sense of letdown when things were over.

"Well, they're not over yet. Still plenty to do." And she pulled back the covers and climbed from bed. There had been a steady…well, um, a steady trickle of cars flowing into town for the past couple of days. Not exactly a stream, but a presentable amount of visitors. Parker's friend, Griff, was soon joined by men from all walks of life.

Both of Ellie's sisters had called her yesterday. "Ellie, you always did get things stirred up," Ronnie said. "When we were growing up we counted on you to get the fires going, and you've done it again. Thanks, Sis. Even if nothing comes of this, it's…well, gosh, it's at least a little fun in our lives. Red Rose has never been this exciting. Look at all these men!"

Ellie shook her head just as if Ronnie could see her over the phone lines. "Ronnie, don't get too excited. You know that the Donahue women don't always make good choices where men are concerned."

"I know that all too well, but heck, Ellie, that doesn't mean we should all just give up. What fun would life be if there weren't men around to bother us and mess us up and make life a little more interesting? I don't have to have a man and be married, you know. I'm not assuming anything like that is going to come of this, but I sure as heck can appreciate the differences between the sexes. Lighten up, El. You've done all the work. Now take some time to just have fun."

Ellie hoped it was as simple as that. She'd always been the mother hen protecting her brood of chicks. Just last night she had called every single one of her sisters just to make sure they were all right. They were all right. She was the one who seemed to be all messed up.

And why not? She wasn't like other women. She'd been the oldest, she'd seen first hand what men like Mick Monroe and Zach Donahue and Avery Johns could do to a woman. Moreover, she'd raised her family and didn't want to go through the fear of that again. She wasn't like all these other women, believing that love was around the next corner.

But when she gazed out her window at Parker's house, she wished she were different. She wished Parker were different, too.

"Aargh!" she squawked. "Get a grip, Donahue. And get to town. This is the day you've waited for. Why are you moping and worrying?"

But as she stepped out the door, there was Parker waiting for her, his arms crossed, sleeves pushed up on his forearms, a drop-dead gorgeous smile on his face.

"Couldn't go to the dance without you, Ellie. This is your party, after all." He held out his hand.

Her heart thundered, her tongue felt thick and useless, her fingers trembled. And as Parker's hand closed around hers, she wished she could stay like that forever. Here, in Red Rose, with Parker this close, all day, every day.

So maybe she was a little more fanciful than she'd thought. These weren't the kind of thoughts she should be nurturing. There was no payoff in sight, no pot of gold at the end of the rainbow, no unexpected wish come true, but for today there was new life in the town. What's more, she was here, Parker was here and tomorrow was tomorrow.

"Let's see what the ladies are up to today," she agreed with a smile. "Sunny hinted at some wonderful and unexpected things."

"My heart stops to think of what Sunny would consider wonderful and unexpected."

"Mine, too. Sounds like fun."

And they headed into town.

Outside the Big Babe Dairy Shop where teenage

girls tended the ice-cream scoops, a tent was set up. Ellie and Parker ducked into the entrance and found Sunny surrounded by men in comfy chairs. Sunny was rubbing one man's shoulders. He seemed to be in some sort of blissful trance.

"Can't shake your hand today, Parker. I've got oil on mine. This here is Ernest. He's a banker, and these others are Jack, Pete and Theodore. But then, you knew that. You invited all of them."

At Parker's blink, Ellie knew that he hadn't invited *all* of them. "I guess word spread," he said, holding out his hands.

"Which only means you did a good job," Ellie said. "Sunny, um...what are you doing?"

"I'm giving massages. Can't you tell? And don't give me that look, Ellie Donahue. You know that I'm a registered masseuse. There's nothing sinful about this."

The man beneath her hands groaned. "It just feels sinful," Sunny corrected herself and directed the men to change seats so she could move on to her next customer.

"This is a great idea," the waiting man said. "I flew in from New Jersey last night, and flying always makes me tense."

Sunny glowed. "Okay, we're fine here, you two. You make sure she doesn't work today, Parker. She's done her share. Now she gets to play."

"Making sure Ellie enjoys herself will be a pleasure," Parker assured Sunny, his eyes sparkling.

The man in the chair gave a long, slow orgasmic groan. Ellie exchanged a look with Parker. She was doing her best not to laugh. Parker looked as if he'd swallowed something and was afraid he would spit it out if they didn't get out of here quickly.

Sunny rolled her eyes. "Okay, I know you two are about to bust a gut. So just get out of here and let me work. At least wait until you're out of range before you let loose, all right?"

But as they stepped outside, Ellie and Parker met Chester coming toward the tent and suddenly Ellie lost her urge to laugh. Chester looked like hell. "She in there?" he asked.

Neither of them answered right away. "Thought so," Chester said. He started to move away.

"Aren't you going in?" Ellie asked.

Chester leveled a look at her. "The woman has made it clear she's not interested in playing with me. Now she's in there running her hands over other men's shoulders. Wouldn't you give up if you were me?"

Parker laughed. "Depends on what you're shooting for. If I didn't know Sunny, I'd give up. But I remember a day when I was about fourteen and she was still working as a clerk at the Dairy Shop. Some man came in and complained about the fact that there was a line and he had to wait. As the man drove away, Sunny put an extra dollop of fudge on the top of my sundae and told me that people who wait and don't give up get extras in life. Seems like that could be useful knowledge to a man in love."

"Love? Who said anything about love? I'm leaving tomorrow." But Ellie noticed that he moved closer to the tent where Sunny was working.

"You took Sunny's advice, didn't you?" she asked Parker. "After you left here, you started your own business and you worked hard to make it on your own merits. You never gave up, and you became everything you wanted to be.''

He studied her for a second. ''I guess I did,'' he said slowly, but his voice lacked enthusiasm. ''You did, too. You stayed here, worked hard and became the most respected woman in town.''

She opened her mouth to deny that was who she was, but he lightly brushed her nose with his finger. ''Let's just agree that we both planned our lives the way we wanted them to be. We can argue later, but for now, I've been given my orders. I'm to make sure you enjoy the day.''

And true to his word, he did his best. They ate from the heaping bowls of food at the picnic, they cheered as Evangelina hit a home run at the baseball game, they marveled at the talent of the barely squeaky elementary school band.

''They're so young and enthusiastic,'' Ellie said. ''Were we that young?''

''Yes, and even worse, we were unsophisticated. That boy with the trombone looks vaguely familiar.''

Ellie laughed. She waved wildly at the band. ''That's because he's Mitzi's son.'' And then, she stopped waving. ''Oh yes, he was the baby you were supposed to have fathered.''

''Ah, the young man who has his father's nose,'' he pointed out. ''And here we are, you and I, without a child between us. Do you ever regret it? Not having kids?''

She looked at him sharply. ''I told you I didn't want a husband and children. Men have never been good to Donahue women, and I have already raised a few children, you know.''

''Yes, I know. You were darn good at it, too.'' And

he brushed her curls from her face, took her hand in his own and led her down the street. He was unusually quiet. Or maybe it was just that they'd left the noise of the crowd behind. Or at least he'd thought so until he heard the sound of someone whistling. The tune was low and lovely and mournful—"The Water is Wide." Parker recognized it and the whistler immediately and turned around.

"You've left all the partying behind?" he said to Griff.

His friend shrugged. "It's a lovely adventure all the ladies have set up here, but…I guess I'm not very good company tonight."

"You've always been good company in the past." Parker noticed that Ellie was studying Griffin carefully. For a second he felt a streak of jealousy flow through him, but then he saw that her eyes were concerned. He'd seen her focus that look on her sisters any number of times. Ah, the mother in her hadn't died even though she might have wished it otherwise if her desire to remain childless were any indication.

"Yes, well, I'll get past my melancholy. I'm just missing my son and wishing that life were different. Maybe Alicia's right and I don't provide him with the things a boy needs."

"You love him, though," Ellie broke in quickly, then blushed. "I'm sorry. This is none of my affair."

Griffin smiled sadly and gave her a small bow. "Well, I've made it your affair by talking about it, haven't I? And you're right. I love that boy beyond belief."

"Then you provide him with the things he needs," she said softly.

He gave a grim laugh. "Tell that to the judge who

believed Alicia's half truths and took him from me for most of the year.''

''That judge is a political hack and we both know it.'' Parker spit the words out angrily.

''Maybe, but he holds my happiness in his hands. He wants proof that I'm a better parent than Alicia is, and she can bring up a hundred incidences when I wasn't there when I should have been. Still, I thank the two of you. For a few hours today, I laughed, I played, I drank and ate well. Your town is enchanting.''

Parker raised a brow, but he refused to voice his thoughts. It wouldn't be right when his friend was obviously hurting so much.

But Griff laughed. He nodded to Parker. ''Enchanting, but I still can't set up shop here, my friend.'' And then he turned to Ellie. ''Thank you so much for your hospitality,'' he said. ''It's been a rather good day, all things considered.''

She held out her hand. ''Come back some day. And bring your son. I'd love to meet him, and I'm sure everyone else would, too. Red Rose might not have much for adults, but the one thing we have is lots of room for boys to run and play in.''

And they both watched as Griff strolled away, whistling his lonesome tune.

''He's a sad man, isn't he?'' Ellie said.

''Yes, but he wasn't always.'' Just as they hadn't always been wary around one another.

''That's a shame.'' Ellie shook her head. They continued wandering and somewhere along the way Parker took her hand. Somehow they ended up at a lonely end of a lonely road. A beautiful place to be with a woman like this, Parker thought. This would be a good place to kiss a woman.

But he wouldn't. Instead, he surveyed the familiar landscape. A bright scrap of paper blew across his path and he bent to pick it up. It was one of the flyers from the open house. He smiled. "I see the ladies were thorough. When they decide to do something, they do it with all their hearts."

Ellie nodded. She didn't need to look at the flyer. She'd had them printed up herself. The Red Rose Café was offering to do catering for corporate events, the flower shop offered plant care services for businesses, there was a new health club at the community center.

"A health club?" he asked.

She shrugged. "A stationary bike, two treadmills and a stepper. Small, like Red Rose."

They had wandered out past the businesses and had left the crowds behind. Parker stopped dead in the street. He turned to her, framed her face with both his hands. "There was never anything wrong with small, Ellie. You know that wasn't why I couldn't stay."

She knew. "You said that your father and your family had become larger than life here. You would never be just another man. You were right, you know. You couldn't be just another man here."

"My family was a big part of this town, but not the best part, not even a good part. My mother once told me that she hoped that I could escape being like my father, but she didn't think I could. I am like him, Ellie. I'm a businessman and in that sense, being like him is okay. I can move around, be on the go all the time, always looking for the next conquest with no repercussions. But here..."

"You would grow bored. You'd start looking for excitement." She whispered the words. "There's nothing wrong with being who you are, Parker, and nothing wrong with being a man who needs more excitement than Red Rose can provide. But I don't think you're like your father. I'm sorry but I never liked him."

Her voice cracked slightly. She had good reason not to like Mick Monroe, and he would never defend the man, especially not to her. He slid his thumbs over her cheeks, caressing, stroking. And then he gave a sad smile. "I'm not bored here, but…I just can't stay. I don't fit in here, and my father is a big part of that. You must have been pretty unhappy that the women of Red Rose voted to put up a picture of him in the community center."

She slowly shook her head. "I was the one who suggested it. He made a contribution. He belonged there. But I didn't like him. He wasn't good to you or your mother. You were right to leave all this," she said, holding out her hand toward the town. "You were discontented here. Now you're happy and successful. I'm glad."

But even though her words were true, she just couldn't smile when she said them. Because while all the things he'd said about her had been true—she was the woman she'd worked to be and she was respected and mostly content—she did have one regret, one big regret, and that regret had a lot to do with Parker Monroe. She loved him, she finally admitted to herself, and because she loved him, she had to send him away with good wishes and no tears.

Sometimes life asked too much of a woman.

Chapter Ten

The town looked and felt as if it had a hangover, Parker thought the next day as he made his way to the Red Rose Café. Litter was everywhere; discarded flyers, food wrappers, an empty beer can, ripped streamers from the masses that had decked the doorway of every business. The noise of yesterday and last night had faded to stillness. Clearly a good time had been had by all, but now the good time had ended.

Cars had been streaming past his door on the way out of Red Rose all morning. Not a man had approached him to tell him that he was even contemplating the idea of starting a business in the town. They'd all left wearing grins, but they'd all ultimately left with no apparent thought of returning. Even Griff had stopped by early this morning to say goodbye.

"I hate to leave you just when things are going to be at their most depressing, but I have to go. Casey's coming back, and all I need is for Alicia to show up and find me gone. She's always told everyone that my job takes precedence over all and that with my constant moving around and living in an apartment in the busiest part of the city I don't provide a stable environment for him as it is. I only have him summers. So, while I'd love to stay and be a good friend, I've got to go.''

Parker had understood. Griff had never been a true prospect anyway, and he felt sorry for his friend. Griff had even worn a smile or two during the time he'd been there. Parker hoped this time in Red Rose had offered him a bit of solace.

And solace was just what he needed to give the women of Red Rose. They were waiting for him. Too bad he didn't have the right words to make this blow to all their plans less painful.

When he stepped into the café, the place was packed with more women than he'd seen in the past. Of course it was a Sunday, not a workday and it was lunchtime. Some of the women had clearly come directly here from church. The patent leather shoes and matching purses were a big tip-off. They all looked so eager. He wanted to ease their minds, but mostly he wanted to find Ellie.

The room started buzzing louder once he got inside. He said a few hellos. He searched the crowd.

''She'll be here in a couple of moments, Parker. She had to pick up her sister. Laura broke her arm somehow last night and had to go to the hospital to have it set, but she insisted on coming here today. All the excitement yesterday just got everyone stirred up.''

He tried to smile, but it was impossible, and when

Ellie came through the door, it became even more impossible. He hated giving her bad news.

Immediately, she looked his way, and he felt as if the world opened up. He would have liked nothing better than to have taken her hand and left with her, gone somewhere where he could touch her as he told her what was becoming increasingly clear. Red Rose was not destined to have the kind of future she'd fought for.

"You all did such a wonderful job," he said, but his eyes focussed only on Ellie. "You worked hard, you came up with good ideas, you did everything that you could possibly do and you did it with style. Any man would be proud to call this place home. I've never seen a town that put more into offering comfort and peace to anyone who happens to wander in."

"I sense a huge letdown coming," Delia said softly.

"Shh, sweetie, Parker's trying to tell us something," Ellie said, moving closer to him, staring directly into his eyes. "What I think he's trying to say in such a nice way is that there won't be any businesses putting down roots in Red Rose. Is that it?" she asked him, her voice clear and calm.

He wondered if these women knew just how lucky they were to have her. Even in the face of defeat, she was steady. He wondered how many men realized just what they were missing because Ellie wasn't available.

He knew, and the knowing was making his throat feel thick. He hoped he could get the words out.

"That's it," he agreed. "It still might happen, but it's not likely. Yesterday I got around to talking to almost every man who came to the open house.

They were all having a good time, but every one of them had one excuse or another why they just couldn't see setting up shop here."

"I guess we're just not very marketable," Ellie said.

He knew she was trying to put a good face on things, but Parker saw red. He didn't want to look at this logically. These were the women of Red Rose whose dreams were being crushed. This was Ellie who had given so much and been given nothing in return.

He slammed his fist down on the nearest table, causing the silverware and coffee cups to rattle. "You don't have to be marketable, damn it, Ellie. You're better than that. You, all of you, have heart and soul and guts and so many gifts that it's a sin that this isn't working out for you. You don't have to talk nice just because I'm here, because I'm just as incensed as you. If I were a man who made products rather than one who simply advises people on how to make their businesses run better, I'd be honored to locate here. As it is, I'll leave the hotel open, but..."

"You don't have to say it. There's really no reason for too many people to be stopping here to stay at a hotel, but some will stop, Parker. It will be a help."

No, it wouldn't. She knew it as well as he did. It would be a bust, and he'd lose money on it, and it would be a depressing reminder to everyone in this town that they'd tried and all their efforts had come to naught. But he couldn't take it down and he couldn't just let it sit again, because either of those things would be even greater reminders of Red Rose's situation.

"I just want all of you to know that I've been honored that you chose me to help you, and I'm sorry that I couldn't have done more.'' He looked out over the room at all these women he had come to know as well as the ones he hadn't learned that much of yet. Lydia and Joyce and Sunny. Delia and Evangelina, Rosellen and Mercy. Ellie's sisters.

Parker blinked when his gaze lit on Chester standing slightly behind Sunny. Chester shrugged. ''I figured I'd stay awhile longer,'' he said. ''See what plays out here.''

Parker wanted to smile, but this didn't seem to be a time for smiling. Instead, he turned his attention to the one woman he needed to talk to alone.

''Come with me?'' he said to Ellie.

She bucked the trend and smiled. ''At least I don't have to discard my coffeepot and apron this time,'' she said as she moved to his side.

''I was getting to like that coffeepot. I won't be able to see one in the future without thinking of you or this place.'' He held out his hand, and she slid her fingers in to rest against his.

His heart seemed to grow fuller. He closed his hand around hers and waved goodbye to everyone with his other, but he didn't say the words. Instead, he left the Red Rose Café for the last time with Ellie at his side.

''Where are we going?'' she asked.

''Good question. Lots of choices, I suppose, and all meaningful. The hotel, the community center, any number of walks we've taken in the past few weeks, but I think…I know where I want to see you for the last time.'' He didn't elaborate, just drove quickly to his house.

''Inside?'' she asked as he helped her from his car.

''No. Up.'' He motioned with his head toward the

backyard, and she instantly understood. She kicked off her shoes.

Together Parker and Ellie climbed to the old tree house. He brushed back a cobwebbed curtain that hid the dusty window, letting in a feeble bit of light. Then he brushed off a small section of the old faded blue rug they'd carried up here so many years ago and invited her to sit. She did, cross-legged, just the way they had when they were kids.

He positioned himself opposite her. "What will you do now that the town's plans have gone awry?" he asked, quietly studying her face. She raised her chin and stared at him, her gray eyes solemn, the way they'd always been.

"I'll go on just as I always have, I suppose," she said. "I'll stick it out and see what happens."

For a moment, he felt a rush of gratitude. The thought that he could come back here anytime, any year and she would be here, sticking it out, was comforting. She would always be here, calm and serene and steady. Always waiting, always giving.

And just as quickly as the thought appeared, it was blotted out by another.

Her serenity, her willingness to wait and to give and to hide her deepest reactions to things kept her apart, kept her alone. That wasn't right. Moreover, it was so wrong. He knew she'd been hurt and betrayed by men all her life, but he didn't want to be one of them. He didn't want to use her, and thinking that he could come back at anytime and take up where he had left off, take her in his arms and kiss her and expect her to respond and to give all that she was, filled him with revulsion.

For a moment, he was glad that she'd fought so

hard to keep herself distant from commitment, because that kept her safe.

And then he wished just as hard that she would find someone to change her mind about relationships because maybe then she would find someone who would shake her calm and make her sing.

He wanted that for her. Wanted it desperately, even as the thought of it happening ripped him apart.

"You're frowning," she said, leaning forward. "Parker, what's wrong?"

He shook his head. "No, I'm not frowning. I'm just thinking."

"About what?"

"About what it would take to make you truly happy."

"I am happy."

"No, you're content. Do you truly want so little in life, Ellie? You used to want more. Remember? Remember how much you wanted this to be special and how hard you worked to make it a reflection of your dreams?" He motioned his hand around the room to the posters and the decorations, the little touches that spoke of a young girl's view of the world as a wonderful place she could treasure and conquer. Instead, she'd stayed here and become a quiet but strong bit of the wallpaper in Red Rose.

"You're frowning again. For me. Stop it. Don't... don't feel sorry for me, Parker. Please." And Ellie reached out and touched his hand. It seared him through and through. It made him want to fold her into himself, but that would be selfish and so he waited for her to speak.

"I did want things when I was younger, but all little girls have dreams. Mine crystallized, matured, settled. Because of the way things were, I suppose. My father wasn't much of a man. My mother? Well, she seemed to be so frail, buffeted by every breeze that blew. I had good reason to dislike your father. Though no one ever spoke of it, I know as well as you do, that he approached my mother. She was rattled, good for nothing for days, so upset that she told me and then made me swear that I wouldn't tell anyone. I'm sure she wasn't doing her job right during that time. Some wives, had they found out, would have fired her. But your mother didn't. If not for her kindness in keeping my mother on, if not for the steady consideration of your family…well, we would have had nothing, been nothing.''

He knew what she was referring to. It was the one time he knew of when his mother had stood up to her husband about his indiscretions. She had been thunderous in her anger, emphasizing that the Donahues had no way of making their way in the world if he brought shame to their family. As an employer and neighbor of the family, they had a responsibility to Luann Donahue and her children, an awesome responsibility. That was when Parker had first realized that he had to keep a line between himself and the Donahue girls. He had to keep them safe, even from himself. And he had to try to distance himself from his father, even if that proved impossible.

''Your mother did nothing wrong, Ellie. My mother knew that. So did I. We knew what my father was.''

''That wasn't the point, though. My mother could have easily become a slap in your mother's face, a reminder of your father's perfidy. And what I learned from your mother's treatment of us is that there is kindness in the world, and that there is value in simply going along and being a steady person, in not creating waves of any sort or wanting too much. I saw that hard work, staying in one place, not letting yourself be carried away by wishes beyond your means, by unrealistic desires, meant you could stay content. You could survive even though bad things had happened.''

But she'd been young when the incident with her mother had happened. That wasn't what had killed her dreams. He didn't know what had. Maybe just the day to day job of being responsible for raising her sisters, maybe his own running from responsibility by leaving the town, maybe just habit, maybe those other men she'd hinted at. Whatever it was, Ellie appeared to have lost her dreams or even the memory of having any.

''Ellie,'' he said gently. ''You're a special woman. You always were. For your sake, I wish I could have given Red Rose the gift of life and the promise of survival. But since I seem to have failed at that, I would like you to have some small token to remember me by, to remember us the way we used to be.'' He reached into the corner and pulled out the wooden box of treasures, the one she'd insisted he had to have.

He placed it in her hands, and she bowed her head, staring at it. ''Do you remember what's inside?'' she asked.

''Some of it. Enough.''

When she opened it, a small puff of dust flew up, making her sneeze.

''Maybe I should have tucked a handkerchief inside all those years ago,'' he teased, and she raised those wide gray eyes to his, a smile in her own.

''Probably you should have, but if you recall, I was the one forcing the treasure box issue. If there was to be a handkerchief, I should have thought of it, but...''

He grinned. ''But you never had a handkerchief or a tissue on you when one was needed. I remember wiping blood from a cut on your arm because you had nothing handy and were prepared to stop the bleeding with a dirty leaf.''

''Unfair,'' she said with a chuckle. ''I was eight and trying to prove I was brave when the sight of all that blood made me want to faint. I figured the dirty leaf would raise me in the estimation of a lofty eleven-year-old male.''

''It did,'' he said, tucking a bit of hair behind her ear with his fingertip. ''You were—and are—so very brave. I've always admired you, Ellie.'' His voice nearly broke on the admission.

She ducked her head and dove into the box. And came up with a pretty pink stone. ''I found this on a school field trip. I remember thinking that it might be a wishing stone, when I still believed in such things. But it wasn't. It was just a rock. I guess I gave it to you, because I thought that all boys liked rocks.''

''I loved it. Great rock,'' he agreed. ''What else is there?''

She fished deeper. ''A Queen cassette. Remember the summer that we went around singing 'We are the Champions' until everyone was ready to duct tape our mouths closed?''

''Yes. It became the club theme song. You wanted to tour the country and win over scores of fans. You had a very good voice, by the way. Do you still sing?"

She winced and shook her head. "Not in public."

Ah, but in private she still did. He wondered if she still fantasized about having the masses adoring her. Which was pretty funny because everyone here in Red Rose did adore her. Parker would bet that if she lived in Chicago, everyone she met would adore her as well. But that was too painful a thought. He couldn't take her with him.

"What else?"

She blinked. "A travel brochure from Hawaii." She hastily put it back. They had talked of all the travels they would take. Since then, he'd been to Hawaii so many times he no longer even thought of how it had seemed so exciting back then, but Ellie…well, he'd bet she'd never been outside the state of Illinois more than once or twice in her life.

"I didn't give this to you to make you self-conscious," he said gently.

"I probably seem pretty bumpkinish nowadays," she said softly, "but that's okay. I'm okay with being a bumpkin. I like bumpkins."

"Me, too," and he gave up on being smart, pulling her close into his arms. "Don't think I want you to be any different than you are," he whispered against her ear. "I don't. I adore you the way you are. I always did. I only gave you this because it was *us*. Everything in that box, we put there. And we were good and happy then. I just want you to remember that and to be happy if times ever get bad for you here. You can pull out that box and remember what good friends we were and to remember that you can call me if you ever want to or need to. Or…or if you want someone to take you to Hawaii.''

She laughed, a small hiccup of a laugh and he pulled away and stared into her damp lovely eyes.

''I mean it, Ellie,'' he warned.

''I know you do. Thank you.''

But Parker could hear what was written in her voice. She would never call on him for any reason. The only reason she'd called him this time was because her friends had asked her to. He wanted to swear. In his mind he did swear, because there was nothing more to be said. He had to go. She had to stay. She wouldn't thank him for even entertaining the thought of staying here with her. She knew what she wanted out of life, and all of it was right here in Red Rose. All the dreams in that little wooden box were dreams from the past. Gone for both of them. Beautiful but no longer relevant.

''Come on. I'll help you down,'' he said.

She nodded, then reached out and touched his arm. ''I'll—do you mind if I stay here for a few minutes longer? It will be the last time, you know.''

Because she was burying their relationship for good.

Parker nodded tightly. ''Stay for as long as you wish.'' He stared at her for a moment. ''Ellie,'' he said. ''Goodbye.'' And then he swept her close against him and kissed her.

She kissed him back and then pushed away. ''Goodbye, Parker.'' And she waited.

He did as he was expected to. He left her. He got in his car and left Red Rose behind once again. Like the legendary Brigadoon, Red Rose faded away in his rearview mirror. And he was on the open road. Alone.

He'd been alone all his adult life, keeping everyone at bay, but not like this. It had never been like this. Because before he had been alone by choice.

And he knew now that if he'd had a choice today, he wouldn't be on his own. He'd be back in that tree house with Ellie creating more memories.

But he'd run from Red Rose before. If he tangled Ellie up with him in a life she didn't want, if he tried to force himself on her the way his father had tried to force himself on her mother, it would be the lowest kind of low he could ever sink to.

Better to run now.

Ellie heard the car's engine catch. She heard the sound of Parker's retreat from her life. Sightlessly she looked down at the treasures in her lap.

And then she gathered them close to her, paper crushing, objects spilling from her arms as she drew a deep shaky breath and held on.

She loved him. She'd always loved him, and there had never ever been the slightest chance that she could have him. It wasn't his way.

These things in her arms, these memories were all that she would ever have of him. She'd coaxed him back to Red Rose once. He wouldn't be coming back ever again.

Somehow she would have to live with that, deal with that.

''And I will,'' she whispered. ''But not now. Not today.'' Today her lips still remembered his touch. She would cherish that memory for a few hours more.

And then she would go on. Somehow.

Chapter Eleven

Parker slammed the phone down again for the third time that day. He frowned at the receiver.

"The damn thing just won't die, will it?" His assistant, Jeb, stood in the doorway, holding a cup of coffee.

Parker snarled at him. Jeb laughed and shook his head. That was half the reason that he'd hired the man. He could snarl at him, and Jeb didn't even care. Of course, he was a darn good assistant, too.

"Why don't you call her?" Jeb suggested.

"Who?"

"I don't know. Whatever woman is turning you into a lower life form. Must be a woman. Nothing else can make a man that miserable."

"Ellie didn't make me miserable. I did."

"Ah, Ellie, the pretty little mouse with the beautiful eyes. The one who came in here and made you dance to her tune."

Parker opened his mouth to bark that he had never

danced to anyone's tune, then closed it again. Jeb was right. No point in arguing.

The phone rang again and Parker reached for it.

Jeb slipped in underneath his hand and scooped it up. "We're losing clients," he mouthed, so Parker let him have his way.

He didn't want to talk to clients, anyway. What he wanted and had been trying to find was someone who could have his arm twisted into opening up business in Red Rose. So far he'd had no takers. Just a lot of hemming and hawing and rejections.

Let Jeb get rid of whoever was on the phone.

But as his assistant continued to talk and talk nice, nicer than usual yet, Parker glanced up at him.

"Yes, Mrs. Arlington, he's right here. I'll put him on."

Jeb held out the phone, and Parker took a deep breath. "Mother," he said. "Is something wrong?" He sat up straighter and gave her his full attention.

"You mean because I never call you and I have today?"

He didn't answer at first. She was dead right about his concerns, but a man didn't castigate his mother for not calling.

Before he could formulate a tactful reply, she laughed. "You're right, dear, I never do call. It always seemed that you valued your personal space and privacy so much that I always felt as if it was best to let you set the pace, but..."

"What? Something *is* wrong, isn't it, Mother? Never mind, I'll be right there, whatever it is." He started to hang up the phone.

"Parker, no! Nothing's wrong. Don't hang up on me," she called, and he eased back into the chair.

''What is it then?'' he asked.

''Well, Parker, Son, dear,'' she fluttered. His mother never fluttered. ''I called because I was worried about you. You seemed so...so lost when I spoke with you last, so different from your normal self, and you were in Red Rose. Going back to childhood haunts can be traumatic. I just wanted to make sure that...well, Parker, Jeb tells me you're very anxious this week.''

Parker leveled a killing look at his assistant. He did not pay the man to tattle on him to his mother.

Jeb pretended to be studying a picture on the wall. He might have even whistled, but perhaps Parker wasn't hearing right. His senses were all turned upside down these past few days. He wasn't focusing clearly on anything.

''Parker, there is something wrong, isn't there? I mean, more than the usual. I knew you shouldn't have gone back to that town.''

''It's not the town, Mother. Actually, I was rather surprised to find that Red Rose suited me this time around. I wouldn't have minded staying. In fact, I would have liked to have stayed.''

''But you didn't, and now you're acting uncharacteristically angry and growling at everyone. That sounds very much as if something happened when you were there. Parker, what happened?''

''Don't worry about it, Mother.''

''You're not allowed to tell me that. I'm your mother, and I can worry. I've always worried about you, but I've tried to stay out of your affairs because you seemed to want it that way, and you seemed reasonably content. But if you're miserable and it's showing in other aspects of your life, then...what can I say? I won't interfere, but I'll still worry."

"I'll get over it, Mother. I don't think that love kills a person."

"Love. With who?"

He didn't answer right away. "It's Ellie again, isn't it?" she asked softly.

"You say that as if she and I were in love when we were children. We weren't, you know. We were friends. I don't want to lose her as a friend. I'm doing my best to stay away from her, to get over her. I don't want to hurt her."

"Parker, that's the last thing I want to hear you say. I've watched you for years, holding yourself distant, trying not to get involved with anyone, but...even when you were small, there was something special between you and Ellie."

"You told me I had to be careful of her and her sisters, and I understood that. I've done that."

"And it was the right thing to do if there wasn't ever going to be anything lasting between the two of you. That was what always concerned me. The two of you were so volatile, anything could have happened, but Parker, you're not volatile anymore."

If only she knew.

"And you're not your father. I used to lie awake nights wondering if you would grow to be like him, I made the mistake of saying that to you once, but you were never like him. Mick loved women for their frailties. You admired Ellie for her strength. Does she know?"

"That I love her? I took great pains not to let her know."

His mother tutted. "She was a strong, intelligent

little girl. If nothing's changed, then she's a strong, intelligent woman. Intelligent women like choices, they like to be in on things.''

He knew that his mother was making her conclusions based on herself. His father hadn't given her any choices. He'd relegated her to a role that it was painful for her to play. But her comment about women wanting to be in on things almost made him laugh. Ellie had always been in the thick of things...when she'd been given a chance.

''Mother, Dad and...Ellie's mother—''

''I never blamed Ellie for that. I just didn't want her—and you—to get tangled up in it. For a long time, Luann and I kept everything on the most businesslike keel we could manage, because it was too painful to do anything else. You and Ellie were young, she was clearly besotted with you, and you weren't ready for that kind of worship at the time.''

No, he probably hadn't been. He had burned hot and fast in those days. He had always burned hot and fast, and he could have seriously hurt Ellie. Leaving had been the smartest move.

''Parker, I don't want to ask this, but I have to. For your sake and hers. Can you be faithful to her?''

It was a legitimate question, one he needed to think about. ''I don't know,'' he said.

''I'm sorry,'' she said. ''But if that's the case, then perhaps you're right to stay away.''

Killing pain streaked through him, so hard he nearly dropped the phone. With an effort he breathed and held on. ''I know that. I'm doing that. I'm staying away.''

''Parker, I'm sorry. I shouldn't have called and upset you, dear.'' Her voice was filled with sadness. She had called when she never called. She had worried. Parker couldn't let her hang up and feel that she'd done something wrong.

"No, I'm glad you called. It's just that...well, I can't tell you whether I can be faithful, because I can't seem to think straight. At all. Right now all I can think of is Ellie." His voice came out strangled, his throat and his eyes and his chest felt tight and raw.

"That's something then, Parker. I shouldn't tell you this, and I wouldn't except that you seem to need to hear it. Even on our honeymoon, your father was looking at other women. I was never the only thing he could think about."

Parker's throat started to close up. His mother had endured many bad years with his father. He knew she'd stayed because of him.

With a great effort he cleared his throat, found his voice. "Well, I shouldn't say this, either, but I will, because I need to. I hope that Edward treats you right." It was the first time he had ventured to discuss the more personal aspects of his mother's marriage. "If he doesn't, I'd like to talk to him. Maybe I should have talked to Dad long ago."

His mother gave a watery chuckle. "It wouldn't have helped. And yes, Edward loves me. And only me. He shows me and tells me so every single day. I'm happy. You be happy, too. Please. You think about what we've talked about, and then...then, you do something."

"I will, Mother."

When he hung up the phone, he sat staring at it for a long time. He and his mother hadn't talked that much or that way in a very long time. Maybe they never had. Perhaps they were doing so now because he was older. Or maybe it was the fact that they had both survived Mick Monroe and now they were both in love.

He'd told her he would do something about Ellie.

Longing and pain rushed through him. He wanted to do something. Heck, he wanted to swing through the trees on a vine, scoop up Ellie and steal her away to be his forever.

But Ellie Donahue was a practical woman. What could he do to win the heart of a practical woman who didn't want marriage?

Was it even possible to do that?

Ellie stared at the nail she had been pounding. It was bent, so she took the claw end of the hammer and pried it out. It was the third nail she'd bent in the past ten minutes. Her fingers were all bandages from hitting them. To look at her today, no one would believe that she'd spent half her life pounding nails.

"I'm afraid I'm going to have to come back and work on this porch tomorrow, Sunny. Right now I'm just doing more harm than good."

"That's okay. Chester's coming to pick me up and take me to dinner and a movie, anyway. We're driving all the way to Des Moines, so I need to go get cleaned up."

Ellie tried to smile. "I'm happy things are working out for you and Chester." She was, too. She just couldn't seem to be able to drudge up much enthusiasm for anything lately.

Sunny leveled a look at her. "There's nothing between Chester and me. The man is way too cocky for my money, but he does provide me with a free night out on the town now and then. I'll take my fun where I find it. Men are pigs, anyway."

Ellie raised one brow. Ever since the failure of all their plans, there had been far too many women willing to spit in the eye of any man that got too near. Rejection was a hard pill to swallow.

"Just look at what that man did to you," Sunny continued. "You can't even pound a nail in a post anymore."

"It's not his fault."

"It is. You love him."

"That's not his fault, either."

"The man would have been a dolt not to see that you adored him."

"I didn't let him see."

"Hmpff! I could see it."

"You're a woman."

"Exactly!"

Ellie sighed. There was no winning this one. Sunny needed someone to blame, and Parker and Chester were convenient. She wished she could blame someone for the way she felt, too, but then, she had always loved Parker. She just loved him more than ever, now, and it was her own fault. She'd known he was not for her. All her life she'd known that, and yet she'd still fallen hard, like a skydiver without a parachute.

"I'd better get going," she said, as she gathered up her gear.

"Guess so. That must be Chester coming down the road. He's kicking up so much dirt that we'll be breathing dust for hours, and he's early, too. Leave it to a man to rush a woman before she's had her bubble bath."

Ellie turned to watch the car coming down the road,

but only saw dust at first. When the car came closer, though, her heart started thumping erratically.

"That car's not Chester's. It's too small," Sunny said.

But Ellie was already off the porch. She started to run down the road, then stopped herself. Why was he here? What would he think she was doing running to meet him this way? With the greatest of efforts, she stopped and waited. She steeled herself to look calm.

Parker pulled up and stopped several hundred feet from her. He climbed from his expensive—and very dusty—sports car.

"Lydia told me that you were out here," he said, but he didn't come any closer.

She nodded. "I—why are you here? You're not supposed to be here."

"I know." His voice told her nothing. He moved closer. "I came to tell you that I have news."

"You drove all this way?"

He was still moving toward her. "I wanted to be with you when I told you."

And she gave up pretending to be calm. "Tell me what?" The words barely made it out of her mouth as she rushed forward and then stopped again.

"You're going to have a new member of the community. At least part-time. Griff is coming back."

"Griff? Your sad friend?"

"Yes. As you made me see, this is a great place to raise a boy. I called him finally, to talk about that. We decided that Red Rose might be the answer to his problems with his ex-wife, at least in part. If he brings Casey here every summer, what judge could accuse him of being a bad father when this is so clearly a perfect place for a child?"

She tried to smile. ''You probably beat that into his head, didn't you?''

''Maybe a little, but you were the one who placed the idea in my head.''

''Well, that's good. I hope his son likes it here.''

''While I was at it, I mentioned that he might find this place good for his business, too.''

She frowned. ''I don't understand. I thought you said that he made sporting goods and that this wasn't a good place for a factory.''

''Maybe not a normal factory, but...that baseball game and the overwhelming response to it convinced me that this might be a great place to bring potential clients, to demonstrate his product. There's so much room, so much land. Griff's already checked into real estate in the area. He's buying the old Manniston place. Lots of room to set up baseball demo areas, field hockey demo areas, football and basketball and badminton and...well, you get the picture. He's going to turn the house into a perfect place for his son and visiting guests and turn the surrounding area into a perfect showplace for his business. He can spend most of the summer bringing in clients and entertaining them to the hilt. When he's done, what judge could look at O'Dell Hall and even think that a boy wouldn't be getting the best of everything surrounded by sports activities and a town filled with nurturing people who will cherish him and feed him and teach him to climb trees? It's a good move for him in many ways. Won't solve all his problems, but it's a good move for a father to make.''

His voice was filled with emotion and he was concentrating on her with such ferocity that Ellie could barely breathe. He had come all this way to tell her this, to give her this gift, because he felt a responsibility toward her, as he always had.

"Thank you, Parker. That's wonderful news." She tried to inject her voice with enthusiasm, but it was so difficult. Saying goodbye to him had been tough. Now she was going to have to do it again.

Only ten feet separated them now, and he bridged the gap. "I'm sorry, Ellie. Perhaps I should have called and told you I was coming." He reached out and touched a strand of her hair, tucking it back into place. She thought that she was going to start crying. She didn't want him to see that, and so she turned away.

"No. No, I appreciate the fact that you came."

"But you wish that I hadn't."

She shook her head, but she couldn't manage to actually speak.

He stepped close. "Ellie, you may not like this next part. I'm thinking of getting rid of part of the hotel."

She whirled then, her voice freed by indignation. "You're not still worrying about your father tainting it, are you, because you just fixed it up. It's lovely and new and fresh and all yours now. You don't have to do that for us. I told you that we didn't mind having it here."

He shook his head and touched her cheek. "After I left here, I wondered what I could do for you, and finally I realized that besides Griff, I could do something more. I'm not getting rid of the whole hotel, just a small portion of it, and I'm not tearing it down. I'm just converting it to offices. I'm thinking of expanding part of my business base to Red Rose."

A million thoughts tripped through her head, none of them coherent. She was afraid to say what she was really thinking, hoping. ''Will people really travel here from Chicago?'' Her voice sounded weak, almost faint.

''They won't have to. I'm only a couple of hours from Chicago. I'll still go there a couple of days a week, but I'll be here, too. Besides, I have a small plane. Maybe I'll build a small airstrip...and a few other things.''

There was a look in his eye, a fierceness, a hunger. She swallowed hard and tried to keep from rushing him and throwing her arms around his waist. ''Other things?'' She suddenly didn't give a hoot about the businesses in the town, the fate of Red Rose. All she cared about was this man, this moment and her fear that he would finish talking and return to his car and Chicago any moment.

Parker shrugged at her question. ''I found a couple of men interested in starting a shoe shop. Handcrafted stuff this time, nothing very big, but it might grow in time. I know how the women of Red Rose love their shoes. Two men isn't much, I know, but it's more than no men at all. Oh, and one more thing, Ellie.''

Her head was swimming. She didn't know what to think.

''I'll be starting a small business of my own as well. I've already got a few workers interested in coming along for the ride.''

''Your own business?'' What was he saying?

He studied her closely, unblinking, never taking his eyes from hers even when a crow cawed loudly overhead. ''Yes. Custom-made tree houses, made to fit the customer's personal tastes. Of course, I don't know how good I'll be at that. I might need some help, some advice, if you'd be willing.''

She tilted her chin up, daring to stare him full in the face. ''You want my help?''

He leaned closer. She wished he would lean closer still. ''I was thinking I'd like a partner.''

''A business partner?''

''Among other things. Oh, I know you won't marry me, El,'' he said quietly, touching her cheek so that she felt as if she were melting. ''No matter how much I love you, I won't ask what you don't want to give,'' he said, sliding his fingertips to her lips in a slow caress. ''But I'm willing to be your friend if that's all you can give. Or if I'm very lucky, your love slave, even if that might seem a bit humiliating to most men. It won't be humiliating to me, because I know I'm never going to love anyone else, anyway.''

He touched her throat and stepped closer, slipping his hands up to cup her face.

She swallowed hard and blinked to make sure she was completely awake. ''You want me to live with you, then?''

''If that's all you'll give me.''

''What do you want me to give you?''

''You. All of you. Forever. But I'll take you on whatever terms I can get.''

She raised her face to his and he kissed her gently. Then she pulled back. ''Did you really just say that you loved me?''

He smiled grimly. ''It seems I do. Not only that, I adore you, I worship you, and damn it, Ellie, I just can't seem to live without you. Don't make me do that.''

''You're staying in Red Rose, then?''

''I'm staying as long as you'll let me.''

Suddenly the flood of feelings she'd been holding

at bay all her life broke in Ellie. She smiled up at Parker through sudden tears of joy, then surged closer into his arms, locking her arms around his neck and kissing him wildly. "If you're staying this time, then I want it to be forever."

He groaned and branded her with his mouth, with his heat. Again. And again.

"Ellie, oh lady, how I love you."

"Parker?"

"Yes?"

"You love me on my terms?"

He pulled back and stared at her. "Yes. Name them."

She placed her hands on his chest and held his gaze. "Will you—do you really want to marry me?"

"More than anything, if you'll have me."

She rose on her toes and twisted up, placing her lips near his ear. "I want that more than anything, too. And Parker?"

He pulled back and waited for her to speak.

She swallowed. "And if we have children who come along, I'll welcome them and raise them with all the love in my heart. I only ask one thing."

"I'll always be faithful. I'm not my father, El."

She frowned. "You think I don't know that? You think I don't realize that you wouldn't have offered for me if you weren't sure that our marriage would be good and right and forever? You've always been true to me, Parker. That's not what I wanted to ask."

He smiled down at her, then touched his forehead to hers. "Name it. It's yours."

"Okay. Let's not wait. Let's get married right away. I don't want a big wedding. Just you."

And he picked her up and whirled her around in

his arms. ''You,'' he said, ''are the answer to a man's dreams.''

She smiled down at him. ''I hope so.''

''I'll prove it.'' And he pulled her as close as two people could get and kissed her. Slowly, deeply, passionately. He molded his body to hers and deepened the kiss. The world started to disappear, and Ellie pressed as close as she could get, her arms around his neck.

A loud cough sounded behind them. ''This is so very beautiful, you two, but I hope you don't intend to prove your love in my front yard.''

Ellie turned to smile at Sunny. ''He loves me, Sunny.''

''Ellie, sweetheart, any fool with half an eyeball could see that. Now, Parker, go take her somewhere where you can kiss her properly.''

Parker laughed and pulled Ellie to his side. ''That sounds like a fine idea, Sunny. I know just the place, and I know just how I want to kiss her.'' He gave her another long kiss.

''Parker, don't you have any shame?'' Sunny asked.

Parker took Ellie's hands in both of his. ''No, Sunny. I don't have any shame. Just lots of love for Ellie, and I intend to spend the rest of my life just being with her. It'll be heaven. Now, I happen to know of an empty tree house. It's not much, but it's filled with wonderful memories and not a soul will pass by or knock on the door. We'll be completely alone. Let's go plan our lives, Ellie, my love.'' He took her hand and started to walk away.

But Ellie didn't move right away.

When he turned to look at her, there were tears in

her eyes. Parker looked distressed. He took a step toward her, but she shook her head.

"I'm just happy," she said. "You really are the Pied Piper of Red Rose, you know, and I've been loving you and waiting for you forever. Welcome home, Parker."

"It's good to be home, Ellie." He smiled down at her.

She smiled back. "Good. Now let's go somewhere and kiss."

Parker laughed and twirled her around in his arms. "I love the way you think, my love, and it seems I always did." And then he led her away. The Pied Piper of Red Rose had finally returned to the woman who held his heart.

* * * * *

And don't miss
MIDAS'S BRIDE
By Myrna Mackenzie

Abigail Chesney needed a father for her unborn baby, she didn't *want a man who inspired passion and romance. Certainly no one like her gorgeous new boss, Griffin O'Dell, who could have any woman he wanted. But when a man with the golden touch met a woman with a heart of gold,* anything *could happen...*

Coming only to
Silhouette Romance
In May 2004

For a sneak preview of this romantic story, just turn the page.

Chapter One

A haven. That was what this place was, Abigail Chesney thought as she drained her third cup of decaf and let the friendly chatter of the women at the Red Rose Café flow around her. Here she could temporarily escape her problems. She was safe.

"The problem is, we may have had a few men moving to Red Rose in the past couple of weeks, but we're still overflowing with women," Lydia Eunique, the mayor and owner of the Red Rose said. "The town still needs men and lots of them."

Delia Sable, who worked for Abigail at Chesney's Floral, glanced briefly at her boss, her gaze slipping to Abby's abdomen before she hastily looked away. Abby almost wanted to laugh. Had she really thought that the Red Rose was safe? Heck, this was small-town Illinois. Everyone knew her business and her concerns. There was no escaping her condition. Out of deference to friendship, no one would mention the fact that she was four months pregnant and unmarried, but they knew, and they also knew that of all of them, she was most in need of a man fast even if she didn't want one. Safe? Well, safe had never been a word she had bothered with in her life. Why start now?

"We don't want just any men," she said, setting her coffee cup down.

"That's true," Joyce Hives, the owner of Hives Honey and Produce said. "We want men who'll make good fathers and husbands and lovers."

Not good lovers. Abby had to swallow hard to keep the words from erupting her mouth. Not good-looking drifters, not men who thought they were looking for love, not men who wanted real relationships. Just the basics, just good father material. But then that was just her. She couldn't speak for the rest of her friends.

"Well, maybe that's what we're getting," Sunny Delavan, a big woman who owned the Big Babe Dairy Shop said. "Since Ellie talked Parker Monroe into coming back to town, there's been a trickle of men following him. And most of them are good." Sunny grumbled a bit as she said this. One of Parker's friends, Chester, had a thing for Sunny, and for some reason, Sunny, who loved most men, didn't want to give Chester the time of day. Probably because Chester saw right through her tough act to the soft woman inside. "Maybe in time we'll all find what we want."

"I just hope it's sooner rather than later," Rosellen January said.

Abby was sure that the comment was made in reference to her own condition, even though everyone was trying real hard not to look at her and make her feel more self-conscious that she already was. Maybe it was time to stop drinking coffee and get back to work. This talk was making her and everyone else uncomfortable. She should just go quietly and ratchet down the stress factor that was rising in the Red Rose.

"We can't rush things and risk doing something stupid. The baby's going to be born whether there's a father for it or not," she said, glancing over the rim of her coffee cup. And there definitely wasn't a father. Dennis, who had lived two towns over, had headed for Alaska as soon as he'd gotten wind of the baby brewing inside Abby. It wasn't the first time a Chesney woman had been left high and dry by a man.

And Dennis's hasty retreat was no secret. For a while, Lydia had posted a dart board with Dennis's face on it until Abby took it down. The darn thing was too big a reminder of her own idiocy in believing the engagement ring Dennis had placed on her finger meant that he really wanted her and all that she stood for. In truth, he probably never really had wanted her. He'd had trouble dealing with her blatant independent streak from the start and had viewed her as a physical challenge, but Dennis had known all the right words, and she'd had a weak moment. Who would have thought she could have gotten pregnant after just one slipup? Certainly not Dennis, it seemed.

Anyway, he was gone, thank goodness, and she was smarter now, and much more realistic. Her baby might have only her to care for it, and if that happened she would handle it.

"That's all there is to it," she said. "Let's just face the fact that I'm unmarried and pregnant, and there isn't any daddy in sight."

"Abby, that's okay. You know we're all going to be here for you and the little one," Sunny said. "But there's more to it than that. Dennis might have been the world's biggest jerk, but you can't paint all the men in the world with the brush meant for him. You do want a father for your baby, hon,'' Sunny said. ''We all know that.''

Yes, they did know that, because every last one of them was aware that her father had left before she had been born and that she wanted something for her baby that she hadn't had.

''Maybe so, but do I look worried, Sunny? I'm a big girl. I like challenges, and besides, we don't always get what we want. Sometimes that's a blessing, especially where Dennis was concerned.'' She'd spent her whole life brazening through. People here expected it of her and didn't fault her for it.

''Maybe not, but we'd like you to have a good, honest steadfast man,'' Lydia said.

''For the baby,'' Abby said slowly. ''Not for me.'' She was adamant about that. Everyone knew that. She'd told them before that wasn't what she wanted. ''No dynamics, no good looks, doesn't have to be a genius and definitely shouldn't be strong-willed. I think one in a family is enough. Just a good, simple, kind man who wants a child and won't mind having a wife to boot. But that's no problem. I'm on it. I've already talked to Thomasina, and we're going to take our time about finding a good fit, so I want you all to stop worrying.''

For several seconds after she uttered the name of the local matchmaker, there was dead silence in the room. Probably it was because in the past few lean years they'd all considered going to the matchmaker once or twice themselves. But just as much of the strained silence was due to the fact that none of them really had any faith in Thomasina's abilities to come up with the right man. Thomasina herself was still single at age thirty-nine, and with the dearth of men the last few years, even the overly optimistic matchmaker had given up trying to fix people up. She'd only ventured back into business a few days ago, and no woman in Red Rose had signed on. The general consensus was that a woman who couldn't find her own man wasn't likely to find one for another woman.

"Oh. Thomasina. That's good," Delia finally said, and Abby almost thought Delia was going to pat her head the way one would pat a small child to make them feel better. "But if by some chance Thomasina doesn't manage to find someone, maybe the new businesses that Parker and Ellie are bringing to town will sweep someone along who'll suit. You know we love you, Abby. And I do wish you'd find someone handsome and charming and passionate and...oh...just perfect!"

Abby closed her eyes to keep from shaking Delia. The young woman always had a dreamy look in her eyes. She created amazingly wonderful flower arrangements for Abby's shop and she was patient and helpful with the customers, but Delia was a romantic through and through. There was no way she could understand just how panicky her words made Abby feel. Abby and her mother before her might have had green thumbs, but where men were concerned, everything they touched turned brown and died. Suddenly Abby needed air. She had to get out of here.

With a clunk, Abby set her coffee down and rose, ordering herself to appear calm as she smiled and turned to everyone. "You all have a great day," she heard herself say, her tone excessively cheery. "I'd like to stay, but oh man, I've got just tons and tons of plants to tend.''

And a future it was impossible to run from, she thought, forcing herself to resist smoothing her hand over her abdomen.

A chorus of goodbyes met her, and Abby turned toward the door just as it opened wide.

A tall, dark-haired man stepped inside, his broad shoulders just clearing the doorway. He glanced around the room, his lazy, sexy silver eyes taking in the room filled with women.

''I hope I'm not intruding,'' he said slowly. ''But I was told that I might find Abigail Chesney here.''

All her friends turned toward her. And then the man in the doorway focused those gorgeous eyes on her. His look was so intent, it singled her out from the crowd so completely that Abby almost took a step back.

She didn't. She wouldn't. No one, especially not he, was going to see that she could be even a tiny bit affected by a man giving her the once-over, especially a man who was a total stranger. She just wasn't going to be a weakling idiot again. The Chesney women might have a penchant for cluelessness in choosing men, but they were also fast learners who didn't repeat their mistakes.

Abby raised her chin. ''It seems you've found your target. How can I help you?''

* * * * *

COMING NEXT MONTH

#1718 CATTLEMAN'S PRIDE—Diana Palmer
Long, Tall Texans
When taciturn rancher Jordan Powell made it his personal crusade to help his spirited neighbor Libby Collins hold on to her beloved homestead, everyone in Jacobsville waited with bated breath for passion to flare between these sparring partners. Could Libby accomplish what no woman had before and tame this Long, Tall Texan's restless heart?

#1719 MIDAS'S BRIDE—Myrna Mackenzie
The Brides of Red Rose
Single father Griffin O'Dell decided acquiring a palatial retreat for him and his son was much better than acquiring a wife. But the local landscaper, Abby Chesney, was not only making his home a showplace, she was making trouble! The attractive mother-to-be had already captivated Griffin's young son, and now it looked as if Griffin was next on the list!

#1720 HER MILLIONAIRE MARINE—Cathie Linz
Men of Honor
Attorney Kate Bradley had always thought Striker Kozlowski was hotter than a San Antonio summer—even after he joined the marines and his grandfather disowned him. Now the hardened soldier was back in town and temporarily running the family oil business with Kate's help. Striker didn't remember her, but she had sixty days to become someone he'd never forget....

#1721 DR. CHARMING—Judith McWilliams
Dr. Nick Balfour took one look at Gina Tesserk and realized he'd found the answer to his prayers. After all, what man wouldn't want a stunning woman tending his house? Nick hired her to work as his housekeeper until she was back on her feet. He never anticipated a few kisses with the passionate beauty would sweep him off his!

SRCNM0404